Christmas

New York Times & *USA Today* Bestselling Author

CYNTHIA EDEN

Chapter One

On the first day of Christmas, my true love gave to me...absolutely nothing. Because he had no idea that he was my true love. What a jerk.

—Noelle

"The Christmas tree isn't straight. It's definitely leaning hard toward the right."

At that rumbling, sexy-as-sin yet ever-so-annoying voice, Noelle Lennon gave a jolt of surprise and grabbed desperately for the top of the six-foot ladder. Of course, the ladder chose that moment to wobble in the most alarming way—probably because she'd just grabbed it so fiercely—and that wobble made her knees knock even more as she dangled precariously on her perch. With mounting horror, Noelle realized that she was about to take a tumble that was going to absolutely wreck her holiday.

The ladder tilted sharply to the left—toward the tree—and she fell back to the right, already anticipating the pain that would come when she—

Fell straight into warm, strong arms. Arms that belonged to her nemesis, Brady Breckridge. He didn't even grunt at the impact, because, why would he? The guy was as close to Superman as it was possible to be. He scooped her out of the air as if it was nothing, held her easily, and Noelle could feel the burn in her cheeks as she shoved her dark hair out of her eyes.

She could also hear a loud crash. The shattering of ornaments. The thud of the tree hitting the wall. How utterly perfect.

"Got you," Brady chimed in, all cheery.

Her head turned. The heat of his touch practically singed her straight to her core.

He smiled at her, showing freaking *dimples*, and his blue eyes twinkled. "Don't worry about the tree," he told her. "I think the new look is an improvement."

Such an asshole. Her teeth ground together.

He kept holding her. He even brought her a little closer to his body and his grip seemed to tighten.

Brady's nostrils flared. "Is that vanilla? And a little cinnamon? You smell delicious. Good enough to eat."

Her cheeks burned even hotter because the mental image that came to mind? *Nope, just stop it right there.* She was not going to slip back into fantasies about Brady, no matter how gorgeous the man might be. Gorgeous *and* infuriating. "Put me down." Like Brady cared about how she smelled. He didn't care about anything concerning her and that was why he was in nemesis land. Once upon a time, she'd made the mistake of crushing hard on Brady—technically, his name was Braden. But she'd given him the nickname of Brady years ago, and the moniker had stuck. Noelle had known him forever and had been obsessed with him for most of that time, until Brady broke her heart.

Just shattered it beneath his size fourteen shoes.

"If I put you down, you might cut your feet on some of those broken ornaments. Don't want to tell you your business—"

"Since when?" Noelle demanded. Brady loved butting into her life. It seemed to be his favorite hobby. Well, his favorite hobby *after* his love for rushing straight into danger. That had to be at the top of his list. Brady was special forces. Top secret missions were routine for him. He seemed happiest when he was in some life-or-death situation.

"I don't think it's the best idea to decorate a tree barefoot," he continued as if she hadn't interrupted. "And you shouldn't be that high up on a ladder without someone to support you." A shake of his head. "If I hadn't been here to catch you, you could have broken some bones."

"If *you* hadn't been here, I wouldn't have fallen. I had just put on the last ornament, and I was going to climb down." Until he'd snuck in with his usual silent steps. The man *never* made a sound when he walked. Half the time she wondered if he was a ghost. He'd snuck in and then when he'd spoken, he'd scared the crap out of her. Maybe because she'd been a little more jumpy than usual lately. *With good reason.* But, back to the business at hand. "I had on heels," she gritted out. "Because I'm at the office. I took them off when I climbed up the ladder." That way, she could balance better.

Noelle and her brother Elliott owned the real estate company in Charm, North Carolina, and she'd been trying to make the place look festive. Was that so wrong? Her plan had been to surprise their employees with the decorated tree, so she'd hung around after everyone else had left the office.

She peeked to the side at the wreckage. *Oh, yes, everyone will be surprised.* Definitely surprised. In the worst way.

"I can help you fix things."

The offer surprised her so much that her head whipped back toward Brady. She almost clipped him in the chin. Missed him by about an inch.

His lips pressed together—sculpted, sexy lips—as if he had to fight a grin. After a moment, Brady schooled his expression. "I can help," he said again.

"Since when do you want to help me?" Noelle's voice notched up because she'd just realized... "Why are you still holding me?" If she squirmed, would he drop her? Unable to help herself, she squirmed just a little.

"Because I like holding you?"

She stopped squirming and gaped at him. "Is that supposed to be funny?"

"Do I look like I'm laughing?"

He usually laughed *at* her. Typical Brady. Noelle huffed out a breath. "Why are you here?" And why had she wrapped one arm around his neck? *For balance. Just to hold myself steady. Not because I like touching him.*

She could lie to herself so incredibly well. A true talent.

"I drove by and saw your car out front. Your car is the only one in the lot."

There was a note of censure in his voice. As usual. There was an exceedingly long list of things in her life that Brady frowned upon. Like when she'd been sixteen and he'd thought her homecoming dress was too short and too tight and he'd *loudly* proclaimed his opinion to everyone who would listen. Or like his opinion on her last four boyfriends—he'd definitely frowned upon them. Four perfectly nice men that Brady had deemed to be losers. Or like her car. Her precious, precious convertible. Brady said the car was a death trap.

The man made his living fighting in war zones. And he wanted to talk to her about death traps?

"You went somewhere," Brady murmured. "And you left me behind. Want to come back?"

She'd zoned out, just because she was thinking of all the ways he disapproved of her. And because she wasn't quite in control of herself, Noelle blurted, "You're the one who left me." *Oh, damn.* This night could not get worse.

But, her statement had been the truth. Brady had been the one to leave. To walk away and vanish on his top secret missions and not look back. Meanwhile, she'd spent far too much time looking for him to come home.

Not ever again. Those days were done. She'd moved on. "Put me down," Noelle ordered.

His head angled to the right. "If that's what you want."

Hadn't she just said it was what she wanted?

"But I can't let you cut those cute toes." He carried her a few feet and then eased her down his body. Slowly. As in...inch by inch until he'd put her on the edge of the big desk that waited in the reception area. "You stay here, and I'll get your shoes for you."

Fine. She'd stay seated on the desk, her legs swinging a little, because there was a ton of broken glass on the floor. The area was such a mess. So much for having a beautiful tree ready for everyone.

I'll just fix it. I'll clean everything up. I'll get new ornaments and lights and the tree will be great.

"Here you go."

She reached for the high heels.

But...Brady was reaching for her right foot. His fingers closed around her ankle, and she almost yelped—almost, thankfully and not an actual yelp because how undignified would that have been?—as he slid the shoe on her foot.

"You've got the cutest damn toes," he muttered.

"I had no idea you had a foot fetish." She also had no idea why his fingers sent a stroke of electricity through her when he was just touching her *ankle*. Clearly, she needed to get out more.

Date more. Have more sex. Because she should not be getting turned on from a man just touching her ankle. Someone was hard up. *That someone is me.*

"Don't have a foot fetish." Brady slid the second shoe into place. "Just have a Noelle fetish."

Her breath caught. "That's not funny."

"Again, am I laughing?"

No, he wasn't, but he was clearly playing some game. Her chin notched up. "How did you get inside?" She'd been sure she locked the door. Sure because she'd triple checked the locks. Part of her new routine now that things in her life had altered.

Because I'm scared.

"I have a key," Brady informed her. "Your brother gave it to me."

"What?" Elliott had better not have—

"He wanted me to take a look at security while I was in town for the holidays, so he gave me an all-access pass to the building."

She got a super bad feeling in her gut. Noelle wanted to hop off the desk, but there was a six-foot-four, two-hundred-pound male in her path. Very close in her path. So close that he seemed to cage her. "Why would Elliott be so concerned about security?" Her voice had notched a little too high.

Brady leaned toward her. His hands flattened on either side of her body, pressing to the wood of the desk. "Oh, I don't know..."

Good. That's good. Because you don't need to—

"Maybe it has to do with the fact that you were almost attacked less than a week ago?" Anger burned in his voice and glittered in his eyes. Icy blue eyes. Whenever Brady got mad, his eyes always seemed to go extra cold.

She kept her chin up. "I wasn't attacked."

"That's where the *almost* part kicks into the equation."

A chill danced over her skin. "I interrupted a robbery." And, yes, at night, right before she closed her eyes before bed, she would still see the guy in her mind. Tall. Broad shoulders. Wearing all black. Including black gloves and a black ski mask that covered his face.

"According to the owners of the house, nothing was taken," Brady noted, his gaze watchful.

"That's where the *interrupted* park kicks into the equation," she retorted, voice crisp. "I was planning to do an open house at that location. When I let myself inside, I found the..." *Incredibly scary guy waiting.* "I found the would-be robber. I immediately ran out." *And he chased me. He grabbed my shoulder, but I sprayed my mace back at the eye holes in his mask.* "I got in my car, rushed away from the scene, and called the cops as I fled." By the time the authorities arrived, the intruder had been long gone.

A muscle flexed along his jaw. "Two days ago, you received a delivery of a dozen roses."

Unable to help it, Noelle gaped at him. "You've been gone for five months." Five months, four days, and three hours. Jeez, she needed to *stop* this nonsense with him. Why had she counted? Why couldn't she get a normal hobby? Her new year's resolution was to take up quilting or something else to occupy her time. But back to the matter at hand. "How do you possibly know so much about my life?"

"Because I make it a point to know." Grim.

"You mean Elliott went running to you." That had to be the case. "He's worrying over nothing. So the flowers didn't have a card with them. So what? It's the holiday season. Everyone is busy. The florist probably just lost the card. Or maybe it was from a secret admirer or—"

"Or a stalker," Brady cut in, voice rasping. "Some asshole who tried to get you at an open house and is currently locked and loaded on you."

Noelle blinked. Chill bumps covered her arms. "You are always so bright and cheery. My own personal Christmas card."

His fierce expression didn't alter. If anything, he looked even more intense. Square jaw. Slightly hawkish nose. Brutally carved cheekbones. How one man could look both extremely dangerous and delectably gorgeous was beyond her. Just a talent he possessed.

"It's been five months," Noelle said. "You go completely off-grid, and instead of coming back and greeting me with an...I don't know...*Merry Christmas* or *Happy Holidays*...you appear and start telling me that I have a stalker. I don't." God, she hoped not. "But your concern is noted."

His eyes narrowed. Blue chips of ice. "Your brother is worried about you."

Your brother. As Noelle understood exactly what was happening, humiliation flooded through her. "Elliott told you to check on me. Not just to check the security here, but to actually check up on *me*. Ugh. This is crazy. I've talked to the police. They are looking for the robber—"

"A man you can't identify. A man who had his face covered the whole time."

"Again, you're being way too bright and cheery," Noelle chided him. "Your optimism is a thing to behold." A sniff from her. "I like to think of him more as...*A man they will catch soon. Or...a man who has fled the area*." Option two was her favorite.

The ice hardened even more in his gaze. "Or a man who might be watching you right now through the giant floor-to-ceiling windows of this lobby."

Automatically, her gaze shot to said floor-to-ceiling windows. And she saw the darkness staring back at her through them. Because it was so dark, she would be easily seen by anyone outside.

She would be seen and so would Brady. Any onlooker would also see their somewhat, ah, compromising position. "It's going to look like we're making out." Her hands rose and pressed against his chest. That ever-so-muscled chest of his. "Space, Brady."

A small growl escaped him. "*That's* what you're worried about? Someone seeing me get a little too close to you?" He gave a hard, negative shake of his head and did not give her the requested space. "Why the hell didn't you contact me the minute this shit happened? You could have been hurt, you could have been killed, you could have been—"

"Uh, how would I contact you?" Noelle interrupted to say. "There isn't exactly a phone number to get you when you go all dark ops on me. Besides, why would it matter? I'm just the little sister of your buddy, remember?" A line he'd thrown at her so long ago. One that had ripped out her heart. "Someone who tags along and gets in the way."

His eyes narrowed. "Don't push me."

She *pushed* again with the palms of her hands. "That's exactly what I'm doing. Look, it's...sweet-*ish* of you to stop by, but you don't need to pull some protective big-brother routine with me." Noelle barely contained an eyeroll. "I have one brother. I don't need two. Dealing with Elliott can be hard enough."

Brady stepped back.

Her hands slipped to her sides as she jumped from the desk. A broken piece of red ornament crunched beneath her heel.

"I'm not your brother," he said, voice still growly.

No, you are not. "I'm fine. The cops are on the case. I'm taking extra precautions." She marched past him, crunching more ornaments, as she made her way toward the broom closet.

"Precautions, huh? You mean like staying by yourself when everyone else has left the office? Great precaution job there."

Her hand curled around the knob of the closet door. "The facility was locked. It was secure. You only got inside because you had a key."

"And what about *outside?* You have to leave eventually. You were just going to waltz out into the night on your own? What if he's waiting in the dark? What if he's hiding out there and counting down to when he can grab you?"

She spun toward him, only to discover that he'd closed in on her. Crept behind her with those silent steps. "What is your deal?" Now her own anger burned. "Why are you pulling the overprotective—"

"*Don't* say I'm acting like a brother again."

Fine. "Why are you pulling the overprotective-*asshole* routine on me? I have mace. I have a taser. I have the sense to check my surroundings before I leave. I'm not going to stop living my life just because of that jerk. It's the holiday season. I wanted to do something nice for the staff here at the office, so I stayed late to work on a surprise." One that had been ruined. Courtesy of the *asshole* in front of her. And, yes, okay, it had also been ruined because clumsiness was one of her attributes. "You've done your due diligence. You checked on me. I'm alive. So, how about do me a favor?" She gave him a smile. One that she knew would hold a brittle edge. "Get the hell out."

Brady swallowed and stepped even closer. "How long have you thought I was an asshole?"

Since you broke my heart into a thousand pieces. "Forever," she said breezily.

"I see." Brady yanked a hand over his face. "That's gonna be a problem."

Why was he lingering? "Glad you're home safe, Brady." Dammit, she was. Worry filled her every time he left on a mission, and that tight ball only eased when she saw him, safe and sound, again. "But it's time for you to go."

His hand dropped. He peeked at her. "Did you miss me?"

Yes. "Why would you ever think that?"

The hand that had just dropped now rose. His knuckles skimmed over her cheek. "Because I missed you. Even more this time than on the missions before."

What?

His head leaned toward her. "Can't keep going on like this. If something had happened to you while I was gone..."

His eyes were on her mouth. The temperature in the lobby seemed to have blasted up at least twenty degrees. And was he leaning toward her?

He...*was.*

Once more, her hands rose, too. This time, they curled around his shoulders. Even in her heels, she didn't come close to his height. The man seemed to swallow her with his massive size. "Nothing happened," she whispered. "I'm fine, Brady. You don't need to worry about me."

"But I do." A rasp. "I worry about you all the time."

He leaned in even more—and they had already been plenty close. Noelle had the crazy idea that he was about to kiss her. Maybe she pressed up on her toes because kissing Brady had been a fantasy that she'd had for longer than she could remember—

"Because I worry, that's why I told your brother that I would pull bodyguard duty while I am in town." A nod. His hand slid from her cheek to dip under her chin. He *tapped* her chin. "I assured him that I would keep you safe and that I would keep an extra close watch on you."

No, no, no. A million times...no. "That's not funny."

"Once more, sweetheart, I'm not laughing."

She wasn't his sweetheart.

"Not laughing, but I am reporting for bodyguard duty." Brady winked at her. "That reminds me...Elliott said you wouldn't mind if I crashed in your spare bedroom. Things will be better that way because I can keep a closer watch on you."

Her mouth hung open. Noelle tried to suck in air, but just wheezed and choked. Brady in her *house?*

"I'm a great roommate, promise. You'll barely even know I'm there."

She would know. Every moment. "This is a bad idea."

"We're friends."

Noelle flinched.

"I have stayed with you before. This will be nothing new." His lips curled in a half-smile that almost flashed his dimples, but the ice still lingered in his eyes. "Your brother is worried about you. I'm in town, I need a place to stay, and by rooming in your *spare* bedroom, I can keep an eye on you. Win, win."

It didn't feel like a win. "You have a giant house, Brady." A big, beautiful Victorian-style home that had originally been built in the early

1900s. When his parents had been killed in a car accident, the house had passed to him.

His Victorian was one of the many crowns in Charm, North Carolina. Like the name implied, Charm was an area to behold. Nestled in the Blue Ridge Mountains, Charm drew tourists from all over the world. And those visitors often made a point of driving by the massive home, a true fairytale house with twin turrets and a wraparound porch.

"The house has been closed down for months. And after the holidays, I'm planning to start renovation work on it. Gonna hire some crews." His stare turned considering. "Was thinking about maybe even listing it for sale."

Her heart rate kicked up.

"Good thing I know some great realtors." His smile blossomed fully so that his dimples winked. "You let me stay at your place, you let me give your brother some peace of mind, and the listing can be yours."

She licked her lips.

The ice in his stare melted.

No, no, that was her imagination. Nothing had melted. She was just tired and edgy and... "You're blackmailing me."

"Absolutely."

Her nostrils flared. "Fine. Stay in the guest room, though it is completely unnecessary."

"Um. Yes. Unnecessary. Because your safety is of no concern to anyone. Certainly not to your beloved brother or to me."

"You can stay," she continued doggedly, "but I expect that listing." More than that, she wanted the house. *I want to buy it.*

"Looks like we have a deal."

She still clutched his shoulders. She was also still up on her toes, as if she intended to kiss him. Not happening. They weren't going to seal the deal with a kiss or anything like that.

They'd never kissed. Though they had come very, very close once. Until he'd rejected her.

Noelle let him go. She backed away. Bumped into the closet door.

"Do we have a deal?" Brady extended his hand toward hers.

Fine. Because *maybe* she'd been a little nervous the last few days. Maybe she'd thought—once, twice, or maybe even seven times—that someone might be watching her. Probably just nerves. Just her imagination. She'd always had an overactive imagination. But...

But it would be good to have a big, bad special forces guy at my beck and call. She shoved her hand toward him. "Deal."

His fingers closed around hers. The calluses on his fingertips were slightly rough against her skin. A roughness that Noelle didn't mind at all. A surge of heat zipped from her hand, up her arm, and seemed to zing right into her heart.

"The glass is pretty sharp. It would be a shame if you got cut," Brady murmured, still holding her hand. "I'll clean it up. We'll toss it away and straighten the tree. I'm sure we can pick up more ornaments so you can have the tree looking even better than before."

"How gallant." Noelle forced a smile even as she tugged her hand free of his. "Aren't you the gentleman?"

No answering smile curved his lips. "No," he replied, voice a rumble. "I'm done with that shit. From here on out, I'm taking what I want."

"Brady?" Unease flickered through her because his gaze was suddenly too intense. His features even harsher.

"It's gonna be one hell of a holiday season," he assured her. "And who knows, maybe by the time it's over, we'll both get exactly what we want."

Doubtful. Considering that what she wanted most...was him.

Chapter Two

On the second day of Christmas, my true love gave to me...two blue balls and one really hard dick...because she was freaking gorgeous and had no idea how obsessed with her I truly was.

—Brady

Sleep was an impossibility for Brady. Noelle waited just down the hallway—fifteen short steps. He knew because he'd actually counted the number of steps between his door and hers.

Was he desperate? Yes.

Was he fucking obsessed? *Yes.*

Was he going to have the longest, hardest night of his life? Yes. Even though he'd gone through plenty of shitty nights in places he didn't want to name. Being here, in Noelle's home, having her so close, was the worst torture he could imagine.

Nope. Not true. The worst thing he could imagine would be coming home and finding out that Noelle had been hurt. Or worse, killed. Hadn't it been bad enough when he'd gone away each time and feared that he'd return to find her engaged—or, fucking forbid, married to some dumbass? He'd known that was a possibility. More than a possibility. Noelle was freaking gorgeous with her witchy green eyes and that long mane of dark hair. She'd cast a spell on him long ago, and he'd never been able to break free. Not that she knew. He'd made it a point of not letting her know. No sense telling her about the hell of his own making.

But when he'd come home *this* time and Elliot had met him at the airport in Charlotte, Brady had known something was wrong. Elliott's expression had been too tense, and behind the lenses of his glasses, anxiety filled his stare.

For a minute, Brady's world had seemed to stop. All he'd been able to do was grit out one word. "*Noelle.*"

And on the two hour drive from Charlotte to Charm, Elliott had spilled everything. The masked man who'd been waiting in the house. The fear that seemed to cloak Noelle's normally outgoing personality. The mysterious flowers. The worry that maybe something else sinister would happen.

"I have her." Brady's response, even as fear and fury had pumped within him. Vaguely, he recalled that Elliot had frowned at him, but Brady had just rolled right on, saying some BS about being her bodyguard and crashing at her place, and being happy to look out for her because they were practically family.

Oh, hell, no, we are not. He was not her freaking brother. Not related to her in *any* way, and he was way past the point of holding back the desire he felt for Noelle.

He wanted her with every fiber of his being.

The problem?

Sometimes, she seemed to hate him. Probably because he was an asshole.

A faint creak reached his ears as he lay in bed, glaring up at the ceiling and trying to figure out how *not* to be an asshole with her. His body stiffened at that little creak, and in the next instant, he'd bolted for the door. Brady yanked it open and rushed into the hallway.

He immediately collided with Noelle. Noelle and her soft curves and silken skin and the super short and skimpy black robe that she had around her body.

She screamed when they collided. A fierce shriek that had surely been intended to burst his eardrums. When his ears stopped ringing, he shook his head and realized his arms had curled around her, and he held her far too tightly.

The way I always want to hold her.

"What are you doing?" She'd screamed a moment before, but now Noelle spoke in a low hush. "Trying to scare me to death?"

His heart thundered in his chest. "I was..." Ah, what had he been doing? "Coming to protect you?"

"From what? My midnight snack attack?"

So he'd gone overboard. The last mission had been a particular bitch, not that he ever talked about the missions with anyone outside his team. He'd come back far more ragged around the edges than normal. And then to learn about the danger Noelle had faced while he couldn't help her...

Get it together, man. Now. Before you scare her even more. Because he'd always had to be careful not to scare Noelle. She didn't understand who he truly was. His plan was to keep it that way. "Thought there might be an intruder. I'm doing bodyguard duty, remember?"

"As if I could forget." A grumble. She looked around the well-lit hallway. "As you can see, though, there's no threat. Just little old me, trying to tiptoe down the stairs and get something to drink."

A smile pulled at his lips. "You still go for chocolate milk when you can't sleep?" An old habit, one he remembered from his days sleeping over at her house when he'd been a teen. A few nights, he'd even joined Noelle in her parents' kitchen while everyone else had been asleep.

Four years younger than him, Noelle had originally just been a sweet kid, the younger sister of the guy who had the foolish luck to become his best friend. But then, over time, Noelle had stopped being a kid.

She'd become a beautiful, smart, and charming woman.

A woman he could not get out of his head.

Brady remembered exactly when he'd realized she'd grown up on him. She'd been sixteen and heading out to homecoming. He'd been on leave, and he'd come in to visit with Elliott and the Lennon family. His own parents had passed away. An accident that no one really talked about, at least not above gossipy whispers.

His best friend had stood by his side and sweet Noelle had gripped his hand at the funeral service. The Lennon crew had always been there for him.

So where else would he have gone during his leave time but to the Lennon house?

And he'd seen Noelle. In the dress that had been way too short and her date had been practically drooling. Good thing Brady had paused to have a private chat with the little prick about how important it was to *always* be a gentleman around Noelle. *Because if you don't treat her with one hundred percent respect, I will kick your ass.* The warning he'd delivered to her shaking date.

"You're still holding me."

Brady looked down and realized that, yep, his hands were still curled around her waist.

"There's no threat," she continued, and maybe it was his imagination, but her voice seemed a bit breathless. "You can let me go now."

I don't want to. But he couldn't very well keep hugging her in the hallway all night. Slowly, grudgingly, he let her go and stepped back. "Good night, Noelle." Brady turned back for his door.

"Why don't you join me for a drink?"

The soft question stopped him cold. "Hell, yes." A growl.

"Sorry?"

He spun around. Tried not to look too eager. Probably failed in that endeavor. "I am thirsty." A shrug. "Let's grab a drink."

Her gaze dipped down his chest. She licked her lips. In that moment, Brady realized two very important things.

One...he was just wearing his jogging pants. He'd changed when he got ready for bed because he liked to be comfortable. He could go back in the bedroom and snag a shirt but...

Well, the second thing he'd realized?

Item two...Noelle was looking at him with interest. Not just interest, but actual desire in her witchy green eyes. She swallowed and her breath caught and Brady realized...*Hot damn. She wants me, too.*

He could work with that. Oh, yes, he could.

***

It wasn't the first time Brady had crashed at her place. Not even the second or the third. Growing up, Brady had spent the night at her home plenty of times. Sure, he'd usually been hanging with her brother, but after his parents had died, Brady had made a habit of staying with her family when he'd come back from his assignments. And, after her parents had moved down to Florida, he'd taken to hanging with Elliott or even occasionally staying at her place when Elliott was out of town.

She hadn't minded before.

She didn't mind now, either.

But something felt different.

Noelle risked a quick glance over her shoulder as she entered the kitchen. *Still no shirt*. Not that she was complaining. Brady's chest was a thing of beauty. How much did he work out? Maybe she should ask, just to satisfy her curiosity. She'd felt his strength when he caught her after that little tumble off the ladder at the real estate office. But seeing him without his shirt...

"Everything okay?" Brady asked as he crooked one eyebrow.

Fabulous. He'd caught her gaping at his chest. *Way to act like you've never seen a guy without his shirt*. Except, Brady was different from other guys.

He was *the* guy. The one who'd been in her head far too long.

Now he was in her house. They were alone. He had on jogging pants, nothing else, and she was wearing her sexiest robe. A deliberate choice. A sexy robe and matching underwear. When she'd put the items on, she hadn't expected him to come barreling out of his room at her.

What did I expect?

"Noelle?" Brady prompted as he crossed his arms over the chest that would fuel her fantasies for days and propped his hip against a nearby counter. "See something that interests you?"

Her lips parted. Was he baiting her now? "I was just trying to figure out what I'll have to drink. It's been one hell of a week." Determined now, Noelle moved with confidence and grabbed her favorite red wine. "Want a glass?"

"That's not milk."

She poured a glass for him. And herself. "That's because I'm not a kid any longer." After putting down the bottle, she lifted his glass and turned back toward him.

"I've noticed."

His voice had gone low. Husky. Sensual. She was not imagining that sensuality, just as she had not imagined the way his stare had heated when he'd looked at her robe. Or the, ah, rather large bulge she'd glimpsed at the front of his jogging pants. She walked toward him. Offered him the wine. "Glad to hear that."

He reached for the wine glass. His fingers brushed over hers. *Hello, electricity.* Her gaze held his.

Need. Desire.

That's what stared back at her from the depths of his eyes. Now the question was, what would he do about that desire?

She turned away. Picked up her own glass of wine. Gulped when she meant to elegantly sip. *Oh, well.*

Next question...what was she going to do about her desire for him? *Play the scene with confidence.* She could do this. "The offer of being my bodyguard was cute, but I understand the real plan." Another gulp of wine. Dammit, why could she not *sip?*

"Real plan?" he repeated.

Schooling her expression, Noelle put down the wine and turned back toward him. "You want me."

His hold tightened on the stem of the glass. So tight that she almost thought he might snap that stem straight in two. Instead, he very slowly lowered his hand and placed the glass on the counter. "You sound very confident of that fact."

Her gaze flickered over him, *down* him, to a rather telling part of his body. "I am." The confident veneer she projected was totally fake. "You could have just asked me on a date, you know. Didn't have to go with this whole ruse of you trying to protect me."

"It's not a ruse. I do want to protect you." But he took a step toward her.

There wasn't a ton of space in the kitchen. Her back was to the island in the middle of the room, and he was closing in. She held her ground. "You also *want* me."

Another step.

Her heart pounded hard in her chest, but Noelle kept her voice breezy. "Once upon a time, I tried to kiss you."

"I do remember the occasion." Another step.

She could practically feel the heat pouring from him. "You stopped me." A painful reminder. "Told me that we would be a mistake. Because I was Elliott's little sister. Someone who got in the way."

He was right in front of her now. "You've never been in my fucking way. I was a dick, and I said that to get you to run."

Her heart raced harder. "Why would I need to run from you? I thought you were the guy who would keep me safe."

His blue eyes glittered.

Don't stop now. She forged ahead, trying to be breezy as she added, "If you're now just absolutely desperate for me, you don't have to invent some excuse about being my bodyguard."

"Desperate, huh? You think that's what I am?"

It was what she wished he was. She wished he'd pick her up, put her on the island behind her, and kiss her as if his very life depended on the act. Was that so much to ask? "Admit it," Noelle dared. "You invented this whole bodyguard business because you just wanted to get close to me."

He leaned in...closer. Put his hands on the island in a manner similar to how he'd caged her when she'd sat on the desk in the reception area of the real estate office. A spark of arousal pulsed through Noelle. He was going to kiss her. She could see the intent in his eyes.

After all this time, would his kiss live up to her expectations?

She had a feeling it oh, so would.

"I am close to you," Brady said, breathing the words almost against her mouth.

He was. Definitely close. She couldn't look away from him. Her head tipped back. Her lips parted, and she could practically taste him as—

Whomp.

She shook her head, wondering what she'd just—

Whomp. Louder. Harder. Very much nearby. As if...as if something had been thrown against her window and then—

Whomp. This time, her security alarm started shrieking.

Noelle jolted as fear twisted with the desire that coursed through her veins.

"I'm close to you because you definitely fucking need me," Brady snarled. "Some bastard is trying to break into your home."

With those words, he spun away from her and rushed toward the front of her house. She gave chase right after him.

Chapter Three

On the third day of Christmas, my true love gave to me...three near heart attacks because some punk tried to break into her house.

—Brady

Brady didn't want to run out blind, so he paused to look through the curtains near the front of Noelle's house. His gun was upstairs, and he could go and grab it before he went out, but that would take valuable time and—

Whomp.

He saw the ball of white hit the window. A snowball? What in the actual hell? Then he caught the sound of laughter. Rumbling voices. Voices that cracked every now and then.

Noelle rushed to his side. "What's happening?" Her robe gaped open a bit. A tempting bit that let him see the upper swell of her breasts as—

Whomp.

More laughter. His jaw clenched. "Some asshole kids are about to get the scare of their lives, that's what is happening." He let the curtain fall as he pointed at her. "Stay here."

"But—"

He yanked open the door, and a snowball hit him right in the chest. The cold iced him as the snow slid down his body.

"Oh, fuck," Brady heard a cracking male voice say. "Let's *go!*"

Nope. They weren't going. Because Brady rushed off Noelle's porch and tackled the punk who'd just thrown the snowball at him. They slammed into the ground—the icy, snow-covered ground—and Brady made sure the snowball-throwing jerk was the one who took the brunt of the impact. He pinned the creep on the ground.

"Don't, mister!" A yell from behind him. And then some scrawny teen was grabbing Brady's shoulder. "Don't hurt Jimmy! We were just having a little fun!"

He could still hear the shrill cry of Noelle's alarm. She'd turned on more outside lights, and with that illumination, Brady could make out the terrified features that belonged to Jimmy. The kid looked to be about sixteen, maybe seventeen, as he peered up at Brady with huge, terror-filled eyes.

"Scaring a woman *isn't* fun," Brady growled. "It's a way to get yourself hurt."

"Oh, God." Jimmy whimpered. "Not the face. Do not hit my face. The girls in my class *love* my face."

The grip on Brady's shoulder tightened. "Don't hit him!" A desperate cry from the guy who had to be Jimmy's partner.

Brady turned his head and saw another teen. This one was small, with shoulders hunching and shaking, and a bulky coat that seemed to dwarf his body.

"I've called the cops!" Noelle's voice rang out before Brady could say anything else. He heard her frantic steps rushing down the porch steps.

The small teen with the hunched shoulders whipped his head toward her. His mouth dropped open as he took in sight of Noelle.

Sonofa—Brady let go of his prey and jumped to his feet. "Seriously, you just had to run out?" After he'd told her to stay inside? But as Brady turned, he saw that she'd at least grabbed a coat. A long, black coat that swirled around her legs.

Thank Christ she's not out here in her robe.

"You might have needed me." She even had on boots. The woman had sure dressed fast. She'd probably had the boots and coat in the closet near the door. She hurried to his side and peered at the two teens. "Why were you throwing snowballs at my house?"

"At midnight," Brady added as he caught her hand and drew her closer to him. Closer and a bit behind him. He didn't trust the kids. Just because you were young, it didn't mean you weren't dangerous.

When it came to Noelle's safety, he didn't trust anyone.

"You called the cops?" From Jimmy. "Aw, man. My mom will be pissed."

"She should be," Brady snapped. "You're lucky I didn't run out here with my gun."

"G-gun?" Jimmy's buddy stuttered. Brady needed to get the kid's name. "But we were just playing!"

"You don't play at someone's house at midnight. You don't play by throwing shit at her window, you don't play by—"

"Brady." Noelle's voice. Soft. Soothing. "You're scaring them."

His head turned toward her. "Maybe they need to be scared." They'd scared *her*. He'd seen the terror in her eyes, and he hadn't liked it. Not one bit.

"Listen, mister," Jimmy's buddy began.

"Who the hell are you?" Brady demanded as he focused on the kid. "Name, now."

"Kyle. Kyle Birch. And we were..." A quick look at Jimmy. "Look, it was just a prank, all right?"

Even though Jimmy was bigger, apparently Kyle was braver because he was the one doing all the talking.

And Brady wasn't buying the prank BS. "You picked her house...why?"

"Brady, you have to be freezing," Noelle said. "You don't have on a shirt or shoes."

The cold was his last concern. He'd just caught the look exchanged between the two boys.

"Her house," he blasted. "Why?" He focused his ire on Jimmy, the weak link.

Jimmy winced. "Because he gave us fifty bucks, each, okay? Said it was no big deal. Just toss a few snowballs and earn some cash."

Brady stiffened. "Who gave you the cash?"

"He hasn't given it to us yet," Kyle rushed to say. "We were gonna get paid after. Told us that he'd send us the money through an app when we were done."

The story got worse and worse. "Have you met this guy? In person?"

Again, the boys looked at each other.

Hell. "I'll take that as a no."

"He just...he posted online, and the address he listed was right down the road from my house." Jimmy pointed vaguely to the left. "Just a few snowballs. I mean, what could it hurt?"

Brady lunged toward the teen.

Jimmy let out a shriek.

Noelle caught Brady's arm. "You're scaring them."

He looked at her. "They scared *you*." They'd done it on the orders of some asshole who was hiding. The same jerk who had come after her before? Brady didn't like this mess, not one damn bit. Noelle might not think she needed a bodyguard, but she was wrong.

Someone was targeting her.

***

The cops drove away with the two teens in the back of their patrol car. Noelle stood on her porch, watching them go, aware that her toes had curled inside of her boots and that the cold seemed to chill her to the bone.

The uniforms had grilled the boys, but the kids hadn't been able to offer up much info about the man who'd contacted them. They couldn't even be sure it *was* a man. Online, everything was so anonymous.

"Let's get inside." Brady's deep voice came from right beside her. She'd felt the rage simmering beneath his surface, but he'd held his strict control in place while talking to the cops. He'd hauled on a shirt, shoes, and a coat to go along with his jogging pants. He kept sweeping the scene with his sharp stare, as if he was looking for a threat, and Noelle had to admit that she was doing the same thing.

What is happening?

She crept inside, and Brady locked the door behind her.

"The snowballs must have set off the alarm. The windows were shaking beneath the impact of the hits, and the alarm sensors in place thought someone was trying to get inside." She was rambling, and she knew it. Noelle glanced toward her den and the cheerful Christmas tree that waited in there. The sight of the tree steadied her a little bit. She was in her home. Brady was with her. She was safe. "A prank."

"It wasn't a damn prank," he growled from behind her. "Someone is messing with you. The cops are gonna continue questioning those kids. They'll keep working to see if they can track down who hired them."

She started to take off the coat, then stopped, realizing she still wore her robe beneath it. She'd been in front of him in just the robe before, but now she felt vulnerable. "Do you think the cops will track him down?"

Silence.

Yes, that was what she'd feared, too. Noelle turned toward Brady. "That's a no, isn't it?"

He didn't speak.

So, yes. A no. "I know it's hard to track people online, and the guy might not have ever intended to actually pay the kids. He just…wanted them out here." In the middle of the night. To scare her.

I want it to just be a prank. But…

She knew Brady was right. "I don't have enemies. At least, not any that I know about. I don't expect everyone to like me, but I'm not some horrible person."

"I never thought you were." He closed in on her. His steps seemed slow. Deliberate. "In fact, I think you're a pretty great person."

Tears wanted to fill her eyes, so she glanced away from him and swallowed. It was late. Adrenaline had her feeling all shaky. And her big seduction routine for the night suddenly seemed very, very silly. Brady hadn't stayed with her because he'd magically discovered that he desperately needed her. He'd stayed because her brother had been worried. Because Brady had been worried. And she was grateful he was there with her.

"Thank you." When she was certain the threat of tears had passed, Noelle focused on him once more. Her hand lifted and pressed against his cheek. The prick of stubble teased her palm. "I'm very glad you were here tonight. Turns out, having a bodyguard wannabe close by isn't the worst thing in the world."

His head turned. His lips brushed over her palm.

She sucked in a startled breath. His gaze caught hers.

They could play this off. Act like the brush of his lips against her palm had never happened. After all, it could have been an accident.

His hand rose. Curled around her wrist. And his lips brushed over her palm again.

Not an accident. At all. "Brady?"

He lowered her hand, but kept his hold around her wrist. "You were eighteen years old when you tried to kiss me, and I told you it would be a mistake."

She did not need this walk down memory lane.

"And ever since then, every time I see you..." His gaze dropped to her mouth. "I wonder how you will taste."

Nope. He hadn't just said that to her. Instinctively, Noelle shook her head.

What *could* have been pain flashed across his face before his features hardened. "Got it. I won't push you. My mistake—"

Screw that. She was done with mistakes. "I've wondered, too." Noelle wasn't going to wonder any longer. She jerked her hand free of his grip, only to grab his shoulders in the next instant. Noelle pushed onto her toes and her mouth crashed onto his.

His lips were parted. Her mouth was open. And the kiss was...

Everything I always wanted.

Hot. Demanding. Consuming.

His tongue thrust into her mouth. His taste sent desire coursing through her. Her body quivered and ached and she rubbed against him in her sudden, frantic quest to get closer.

Sometimes, you could dream about something. You could fantasize about it. And you could be sure that the reality of the experience would never, ever live up to your expectations.

A moan built in her throat as her nails bit into his shoulders. Kissing Brady was far, far better than any dream she'd had. In fact, it felt like an absolute fantasy come true...because it was.

He tasted rich and decadent. His tongue teased and tormented. He had her aching and quivering, and her body rubbed against his because she wanted to get as close to him as she could.

When he growled, the sound just heightened her arousal. She fought the urge to rip off his clothes. Rip off hers. To give in to the desire that churned so strongly between them and—

He let her go.

It took a moment for that act to register. *He let her go.* Noelle's breath came too quickly. Her heart raced too hard. Her panties were wet, just from a kiss because she was that turned on. And he'd simply let her go.

"That's why," he growled, "I knew I had to stay away when you were eighteen."

She didn't get it. Probably because her brain was a wee bit foggy.

"I want you too much." His voice rumbled and rasped and seemed to scrape along her nerve endings in the best possible way. "You weren't ready for me back then."

She was the one who got to decide what she was ready for.

His hands fisted at his sides. "Not sure you're ready for me now."

Anger shoved past her desire. "You have no idea what I'm ready for." Her hair slid over her shoulder as she straightened her spine.

"Noelle..." A warning. "I've held onto my control for years. If it breaks..."

Let it. "Maybe you're not ready for me." Her gaze raked over him. *Oh, yes, he is ready.* Clearly, very ready. And large. Her gaze jumped back up to meet his. After a quick swallow, she continued, "Maybe you can't handle me." A deliberate taunt. She wanted his hands on her again. Wanted his mouth. Wanted him.

But he'd pulled away and spewed some BS about being ready.

Brady shook his head. "You don't understand."

No, she didn't. Her night had been crazy, and she could still taste his kiss. "Are you playing some kind of game with me?"

"What?" His jaw dropped, only for him to hurriedly snap it closed.

"You kiss me one moment, then pull away the next. I'm not the one who stopped. *You* did." She huffed out a frustrated breath. "New rule. Don't ever kiss me again unless you one hundred percent mean it." Noelle spun on her heel. This night just sucked.

"I *did* mean it."

She stopped in the doorway. *Don't say it. Don't say it...*She opened her mouth and said, "Fine. Then how about this?" Noelle glanced over her shoulder. "Don't kiss me again unless you're ready to do *more* than kissing." Noelle knew exactly what she wanted. It was the same thing she'd wanted for years. Him.

His eyes glittered. "Once we cross that line, we can't ever go back."

"Go back to what? Being frenemies?" Was that even the word to describe them? "Being carefully, almost excruciatingly polite around each other? Walking on eggshells?" She turned to fully face him. "Because let's be honest. You and I aren't exactly best friends. Sometimes, I'm not even sure you like me."

Surprise flashed on his face. "Of course, I like you."

There was no "of course" about it in her book. "You spend most of your time glaring at me. You leave for months at a time, and you don't ever write to me."

"You *wanted* me to write?"

Was he serious? She took a step toward him, then caught herself. "I do like to know if you're alive or dead. Call it a quirk I have."

"And I want to know about you." Deep. Low.

Was that true? "When we are together, when you come to my brother's place for events or we all get together for whatever random event is occurring, you barely speak to me."

"Because sometimes you have a dumbass date at your side." He stalked toward her. "And I'm trying not to punch the guy, grab you, and carry you off into the night. Keeping conversation to a minimum is how I keep my control."

What? Now it was her turn to have her jaw drop. "Excuse me?"

Brady stood right in front of her. "You really don't get it, do you?" His hand lifted. His fingers slid under her chin. His thumb brushed over her lower lip.

A shiver skated down her spine. Odd, because she didn't feel cold. Quite the opposite. "How about you just spell things out for me?"

"I want you."

That was pretty clear.

"I've wanted you for far too long. When you were eighteen years old and you wanted to kiss me, walking away from you was one of the hardest things I've ever done."

Back to that, were they? Back to rehashing one of the most embarrassing moments of her life. She'd caught him under the mistletoe at a party. Been so nervous. She'd pointed up. Smiled at him, and stuttered out that, "W-we have to kiss now. I think it's a rule." Noelle could feel her cheeks burn at the memory.

Brady hadn't spoken. He'd looked at her. Looked up at the mistletoe. Looked back at her. His stare had been so intense. So *angry*. A muscle flexed along his jaw right before he'd turned and marched away, leaving her all alone beneath the mistletoe. Later, he'd found her and delivered the unforgettable line about her just being the sister of his buddy, someone who tagged along and got in the way.

She'd hated mistletoe ever since. The freaking stuff was poison and why people wanted to use it as some festive holiday decoration was beyond her. "If it was so hard," Noelle forced herself to say as her lips feathered against his thumb, "then why did you do it?"

He released her. "Because—"

"Do *not* say I wasn't ready."

"Do you have any idea of the things I want to do to you?"

That sounded promising. But they needed to tackle the topic at hand. "If you didn't want to kiss me, you just didn't want—"

"I don't want to stop with a kiss. Not with you. I want to strip you. I want to fuck you. I want to have you scream my name until you go hoarse."

That felt like...a lot. Certainly doable, though. She was up for the challenge.

"One night will not be enough," he continued with a warning tone in his sexy voice. "Not even close. When I have you, you will be *mine*. I don't give up what belongs to me."

It was hot in that room. She fanned herself with one hand.

"You had a different life waiting for you. So did I. If I'd kissed you back then..." Brady swallowed. "Well, your brother would have slugged me, but I wouldn't have cared. You would have been worth the hit. I pretty much think you'd be worth anything."

That was...her lips curled. *Nice*.

"I've done things, seen things, that would terrify you."

Her smile faltered.

"I like danger. I'm too well acquainted with it. My life has been about battles and death. Your world and mine are very far apart."

They didn't seem far to her. Only inches separated Noelle and Brady.

"I wanted you to have everything good in the world. *I* am not part of that goodness."

Why would he say that?

"You deserved better than me. I knew it back then, so I walked away." His hands fisted at his sides. "I still know it now. I know I should keep my hands off you."

But he hadn't. Instead, this time, he'd kissed her. Her head tilted. "Why didn't you?"

"Because I have never wanted anyone the way I want you." Gritted. "I tried to give you time. I tried to give you space. Even though I was so fucking afraid—I *dreaded* the day I would get a call or a letter from your brother with news that some lucky bastard had put a ring on your finger."

That hadn't happened. She'd dated. Had relationships, yes, but nothing that had ever felt right.

"Instead, I came home and found out that some SOB in a ski mask had chased you out of a house." His lips thinned. "No one gets to scare you. No one gets to hurt you."

"So you made yourself my protector."

"I've been protecting you for years, you just didn't realize it."

That was ambiguous. "Protecting me...from you?"

He didn't speak.

"I don't need protecting from you." Of this, she was certain.

"Don't be too sure about that." Now he was the one to walk away. "Gonna go check outside. Get some sleep. I'll make sure nothing can hurt you tonight."

Right. Sure. Totally possible to just hop in bed and go to sleep after this conversation.

So going to happen.

Never in a million years.

Chapter Four

On the fourth day of Christmas, my true love gave to me...four hours of sleep. Because that's all I managed to get since I was tossing and turning and thinking about him all night long. Meanwhile, I bet he slept like a freaking angel.

—Noelle

"Are you ready for the big date?"

Noelle blinked blearily at her computer screen before turning her head toward the man who'd just entered her office. Rowen Welch smiled at her, flashing a practiced and polished grin. His thick, blond hair fell lightly over his forehead, but she suspected the casual look was something he'd actually spent a great deal of time working to achieve.

She bit her lip as her mind absolutely blanked in response to his question.

He kept smiling.

"The date?" Noelle finally had to ask.

His smile lost a little wattage. "Yes. The date? Tonight?" He strolled toward her desk and pointed at Noelle. "You're Mrs. Claus, and I'm Santa. We arrive, we do our bit and—"

"You're talking about the charity event?" Now things made sense except she hadn't been thinking of it as a date. Not at all. Because it wasn't.

The real estate company sponsored the charity fundraiser every year. She usually was either Mrs. Claus or an elf, and the other employees would take different roles, too. Her brother liked to don green face paint and act like his heart was growing three times its normal size as he greeted everyone who came through the doors for their big night.

Rowen had only joined the company about a month ago. Since that time, he'd asked her out twice. She'd declined both times. And this was *not* a date, so why would he think—

"You don't have anyone else to be Santa since Carlos came down with the flu. I asked around, and no one else wanted the job." He put his hands on her desk and leaned forward. His hazel eyes glinted. "So we can go as a couple, it will be a fun date—"

"What date?" A hard, drawling voice demanded from her doorway.

Rowen stiffened.

Noelle jumped to her feet. She knew the owner of that voice—she'd recognize Brady's voice anywhere, any time. "It's not a date."

"Good to know." Brady crossed his arms over his chest.

Rowen spun to face him. "Look, we are in the middle of a private—"

"It's for the company's charity event," she added at the same time. "I need someone to be Santa because the man who was slated to wear the red suit came down with the flu."

"My Friday nights are usually a whole lot more exciting," Rowen said with a roll of his shoulders. "But I was telling Noelle that I could make the sacrifice and help her out since she needed me—"

"I'll do it," Brady cut in.

She blinked. "You will?"

"Sure." He shrugged. "You need a Santa. I need to stay close to you. Consider me your man."

Had there been a slight, possessive emphasis on that *your*? Noelle thought there might have been.

Rowen was busy sputtering. He finally managed, "Unnecessary, I can certainly—"

"No, no, I insist." Brady sent him a sharp smile. "You go have your exciting night. Wouldn't dream of taking fun away from a guy like you. I'll be the one she needs. Count on it."

Well, the tension in her office certainly seemed to thicken. "Elliott has the Santa costume," she told Brady. "You can go get it from him."

"I'll do that." Brady didn't move.

He and Rowen had locked eyes.

She wanted to roll her eyes. They were both acting so weird.

"Don't think I got your name," Rowen finally said. He took a few lurching steps toward Brady. Not his usual smooth style at all. He held out his hand. "I'm Rowen Welch. And you are—"

"Brady."

Just that. Nothing else.

Rowen's fingers closed around Brady's in a fierce shake. "You a new client?"

"Nope." Brady released him.

"A new agent then?" A nod from Rowen. "Welcome to the company. I was the new agent on deck just a month ago—"

"Not an agent."

"Then why are you here?" Rowen's voice had lost a little friendliness. Not that he'd had a whole lot to begin with.

Brady repositioned himself so that he could put his gaze straight on Noelle. "I'm here for her."

***

"You're gonna be Santa?" Laughter exploded from Elliott. "You? You barely even put up a Christmas tree!"

Actually, he hadn't put up one. Not in the last three years.

"You don't holiday shop," Elliott continued as he seemingly made his way through a list. "At all."

Not true. "I give you a bottle of whiskey every year. If that's not holiday shopping, what is?"

"You don't—"

"Do you have the costume or not?" Brady groused.

Elliott heaved up a box from beside his desk. A white beard dangled on the right edge. "Oh, I've got it." More laughter. "I cannot wait to see you dressed up. You *do* know that part of the night is spent letting people pose with you for pics? Adults, kids, they'll all be coming to see Santa to tell him what they want this year." He plopped the box on a nearby chair. The beard fluttered to the floor. *"You* have to be jolly. You have to be in high spirits. You have to make their holiday dreams come true." More laughter. "You are going to be hilarious."

"I am so glad that I can amuse you." Mental note—his best friend was an asshole. But then, so was Brady and that was probably why the two men got along so well. He began to poke around in the box. "Who was the dick in her office?"

"Say again?" Elliott seemed to be choking.

He'd found the battered black belt. And a giant red hat. "The dick," he repeated, "in her office. Trying to act like he was doing Noelle a favor by playing Santa at a freaking *charity* event. Who does shit like that?"

Silence.

His head lifted. Turned toward Elliott.

Elliott wasn't laughing any longer. He appeared to be gawking.

"What?" Brady demanded.

"You sound jealous."

Fuck. He did. He was. "Just making up my list of suspects."

"Suspects?" Elliott's dark eyebrows rose. "I thought the cops had the suspects in custody. Two punk kids who are probably terrified and will be grounded for the rest of their lives by seriously pissed parents."

A hard, negative shake of Brady's head. "Someone hired those kids."

"To play a prank, right. Sure, they—"

"To *scare* her." He turned away from the box to fully face his friend. "I don't like it. No one should scare her."

Elliott tapped his chin. "Noted. You don't like people scaring Noelle. You don't like dicks being in her office...what *do* you like?"

Again, such an asshole. "I'm just saying it was a good thing I was at her place last night. Don't worry, I'll keep staying there for the foreseeable future so that she feels safe."

If possible, Elliott's eyes widened even more.

"Now, who was the dick in her office?" Brady demanded because he still hadn't gotten his answer. Okay, fine, so he technically had a name already. *Rowen.* But what Brady really wanted to know was... "Why did the guy think he was dating Noelle? You told me she wasn't dating anyone." When Brady had asked, as he always asked when he got stateside again.

Elliott's still wide eyes gleamed. "I was super worried. Thanks for staying so she can feel *safe.*"

"Someone has to watch over her." Obviously, Elliott wasn't taking this shit seriously. "Have you forgotten the jerk in the ski mask? He could have hurt her. He could be the one who hired those kids."

"Again...why? Why would a robber want some kids throwing snowballs at her place?"

"To scare her! Maybe you have some creep who is obsessed with Noelle." His hands fell to his sides and his voice hardened as Brady warmed to the topic. "He thinks he can scare her, get close to her..." He thought of the dick in her office. "Maybe act like her hero in order to get her to fall for him."

A cough broke from Elliott. One that sounded fake. "Wouldn't *you* be doing those things?"

What the hell? "I would *never* scare her."

"But you are close to her. Staying in her house...and there is a Santa suit—*an actual Santa suit*—that the man I think of as a modern Ebenezer Scrooge is planning to wear so that my sister can pull off the charity event she loves so much." Another cough. "Would you be trying to make Noelle fall for you? After all these years of pushing her away, are you finally trying to pull her close?"

Shit. "What if I am?"

In an instant, Elliott's wide eyes turned to slits.

Yeah. He's gonna punch me. Worth it, though.

"When do you head out on another mission?" Elliott asked. "The first of the year? Before Valentine's Day? When will you be heading out and not looking back?"

"First, I *always* look back." Just so they were clear. He did look back. Over and over.

"Um, is that why you ask incessantly about who Noelle might be dating whenever I talk to you and you're on a mission?"

His back teeth ground together. "And, second, I'm done."

Elliott blinked. "Done?"

"I'm going civilian." A change that he'd been thinking about for a long time. "Gonna do private security work. Already got some leads set up with my buddy, Eric Wilde. I'm coming home." Technically, he wasn't *coming* home. He was home.

His best friend didn't say anything. The minutes ticked past. The waiting killed Brady. "If you're going to hit me, I should tell you that I will only give you three free punches." Who was he kidding? Not like he'd hit back at Elliott. If he beat up Noelle's brother—and he would, because Elliott couldn't fight worth a shit—then Noelle would just get upset, and Brady didn't want that.

"Hit you?" Elliot's right hand fisted. He glanced down at it as surprise slid across his green-painted features. "That what you think I'm going to do?"

Yep. A punch appeared to be a certainty. "I'm planning to date your sister." Saying those words seemed to take a weight off Brady's shoulders, even if they brought him a black eye. "I know that probably pisses you off. I know I'm not good enough for her. I know I should stay the hell away." A long exhale. "I tried to stay away. Thought what I felt for her—thought it would *go away* if I was away, but it hasn't, and I know I'm wrong for her. I get that she needs someone who is as happy and good as she is." He looked over his shoulder. Glared at the Santa suit. "Someone who puts up damn trees and sings carols, and even though it almost physically hurts me, I am trying to be that guy." For her.

"You're...planning to sing carols?"

Brady's head snapped back toward Elliott. "Are you choking?" Because it had sounded like he was. The guy sure seemed to be having lots of trouble. "Hey, look, I heard someone at the office has the flu. You keep coughing and choking. Maybe you're coming down with something." He took a step back.

Elliott's eyes did seem to be watering. He blinked again, quickly, even as he bit his lower lip. "Uh, uh." A shake of his head. "Not sick at all."

"Then what is the deal?"

A smile stretched across Elliott's face. "Just...carols, huh? You're planning to sing carols?" Laughter boomed.

"Just hit me already." The punch would be less painful.

Elliott nodded. "Right." He lumbered forward—and hugged Brady.

Brady's muscles locked down. "What in the hell are you doing?" Elliott was supposed to give him a punch, not a hug.

"I love you, man."

"*Elliott...*"

Elliott eased back a step. Grinned at him. "You're my best friend. I happen to think you are a pretty great guy—you sure saved my ass more times than I can count—but I think you *know* a whole lot less than you think." He squeezed Brady's shoulder with one hand before letting go. "About damn time. I was starting to wonder if you'd ever get over your fear and get moving."

Your fear. "What are you talking about?" Nope, they needed to back up. "Why aren't you punching me?"

"Because maybe I want my sister to be with a guy who would move heaven and hell to keep her safe. Maybe I want her protected all the time— why else would I suggest that you stay at her place to look out for her?"

Brady swiped a hand over his face. "You're playing matchmaker? You're *fine* with me wanting to date Noelle?"

Elliott's head tipped to the right. "That what you want to do? Date her?"

Why hold back? "I want to put a fucking ring on her finger, marry her in the fastest ceremony possible, and spend the rest of my life trying to make her smile." Seemed like good goals.

Appearing Cheshire-cat satisfied, Elliott nodded. "Thought so. Why else would you wear the Santa costume?" He turned away and headed for the chair behind his desk. The leather squeaked when he sat down. "It's really about time, too. Do you know how worried I was that she'd wind up with some dick like Rowen?"

Brady growled.

"Exactly. Now, how about you start practicing your *ho, ho, ho* routine. Oh, and about the Christmas carols? Her favorite is *The First Noelle,* of course."

Like he didn't know that. When it came to Noelle, he remembered everything she liked. A handy talent because he was gonna have to use that knowledge to his advantage. Noelle thought he wanted her. And he did. Oh, yes, hell, yes, he did.

But more than that, Brady wanted her to fall for him. A much trickier deal. One that would require considerable work. Because being with Noelle wasn't just about sex—one of the reasons he tried so hard to keep his control with her. *Not just fucking.*

He wanted Noelle to love him. In order for that to happen, he had to convince her that he was more than just a danger and adrenaline junkie.

Brady slapped the Santa hat on his head and got busy with his *ho, ho, ho-ing.*

Chapter Five

On the fifth day of Christmas, my true love gave to me...five hours of sitting in a scratchy, smelly Santa suit while everyone in the building told me their Christmas wishes. Anyone want to know what I want? Simple...her. I want Noelle.

—Brady

"Bah humbug." Brady yanked off his Santa hat and maneuvered through the packed crowd as he tried to find—

"I think you meant to say, 'ho, ho, ho' instead," Noelle murmured.

He stopped in his tracks and slowly turned toward her. While his costume was old and rough, she looked like the best Christmas dream in the entire world.

She wore red tights, a red sweater and skirt that hugged her deliciously, cute black boots that actually curled at the toes—like elf shoes—and a jaunty red hat perched on her head. She smiled a bit nervously at him. "I know it can be a lot," Noelle said as she put her hand on his arm. "And some of the big wigs making donations are a lot to handle."

The big-money people? Yeah, plenty of them were jerks. And the women in their dripping diamonds had tried to get a little too friendly when they'd sat in Santa's lap.

"But we bring in so much needed money—and presents—for the community. If you come back for the actual distribution, and you see the look on the kids' faces when they get presents that are selected and wrapped just for them, you'll understand that it's worth it. Anything is worth that joy." Her face seemed to light up.

Looking at her, he felt joy. Like he pretty much always did when he was near Noelle. Brady swallowed and struggled to figure out what to say as her fingers curled around his arm.

She glanced down at her hand. Her eyes widened, as if she hadn't even realized she'd reached out to hold him. "But you might not want to come back. I'm sure you're busy, and I certainly appreciated the help tonight." Her hand jerked away from him. "There's a changing room to the right." Noelle pointed down the empty hallway. "You can use it to ditch the costume. I bet you'll feel a whole lot better after you do."

He caught her hand. "I'll be here for the distribution."

Her smile bloomed again.

"I'll be here for anything you need," he added. Yep, Brady hoped she'd get the double meaning on that one.

"That's so wonderful! Thank you, I—"

"Well, isn't that sweet," a woman's amused but cool voice chimed in. "Santa and Mrs. Claus are under the mistletoe together."

Noelle's body jerked. Then her head snapped back as she looked up. An expression of absolute horror crossed her pretty face as she stared above them. Then she stumbled away in a retreat, definitely moving *out* of the mistletoe range.

"No? Not in the mood for a kiss?" The woman laughed. "I can certainly step in to do the deed. Happy to help out." The bells around her wrists jingled as she advanced.

Addison Lane. One of the ladies who'd come to tell Santa what she wanted that year as he sat on the big, black throne of a chair and tried to spot Noelle in the crowd. Noelle hadn't come to see him during his Santa duty, despite his most fervent of wishes.

"He doesn't need help, Addison," Noelle chimed in to say. "But trust me, we all appreciate how much of a giver you are."

Addison's gaze cut to Noelle.

"Addison works at another real estate company in town," Noelle explained. "Addison, have you met Brady Breckridge?"

"Only if you count when I sat on his lap." Addison winked at Brady.

He saw Noelle roll her eyes.

"Brady Breckridge..." Addison seemed to taste his name. "Don't you own that delightful

Victorian on the edge of town? Such a big house for a man who is...single?"

He tugged off his beard. "The house is Noelle's."

Addison gaped.

Noelle looked back at him. A little furrow appeared between her eyes.

"I mean, the listing is hers." Truth be told, he'd always kind of imagined Noelle living in the house, with him. But this wasn't the moment to get into all of that.

"Isn't that wonderful for her?" Addison's voice had turned brittle. She slid a card from her bag and grabbed Brady's hand. Pressing the card against his palm, she said, "If you decide you want more of a shark on your side, call me." She glanced upward and a slow smile curved her plump lips. "Oh, I guess I'm under the mistletoe now." Her gaze returned to him. "And I'm not the type to run away."

Run away? His gaze darted past her. Sure enough, Noelle had turned away and was cutting through the crowd. *Running?* Dammit. "Noelle!" Brady chased after her.

***

Jealousy sucked. She did not handle it well, even though Noelle should have been used to the emotion by now. She'd certainly felt the painful bite a few times over the years when she'd seen Brady with other women.

Addison wants him. The woman's expression had been clear to read, and then when she'd sidled under the mistletoe to get close to Brady—*too much*. Noelle hadn't been able to witness another moment.

A strong, black-gloved hand closed around her wrist. "Why are you running from me?"

She stopped in her tracks as Brady's voice washed over her. Warm. Deep. Sexy. Her head turned so she could glance back at him. A man should not be that gorgeous in the old, thick Santa suit. The red should look garish, and the fake white fur should seem silly. Only, it didn't. Because the red just somehow made his tan skin glow even more and his blue eyes didn't twinkle— nope, no twinkle there—but they gleamed with fierce intent. He gripped the white beard and his hat in his other hand, and his thick, dark hair appeared tousled and sexy.

He *always* looked sexy. That was the problem. To her, he'd always been hot.

Now she was sexually attracted to Santa. How wonderful.

"Noelle?"

Clearly, she should speak and not gape. "I wasn't running." More like she'd been getting away from the mistletoe. Taking appropriate steps to distance herself from the poison that brought up painful memories. "It's warm in here, and I needed to get some air." Her gaze swept over him. "Thought you wanted to change."

"I do, but I want you more."

Her heartbeat raced. "Excuse me?"

He tugged her closer. "Why didn't you kiss me under the mistletoe?"

The question she'd had for him, years ago. This time, though, she'd been the one to retreat.

"Want me to be your dirty secret?" Brady added, as his voice wrapped around her with a dark seduction. "That it? That why you turned and left when Addison started asking her questions about us? Because you don't want anyone to know about what's happening between us?"

The house is Noelle's. "I was hot. I just needed air."

His head came even closer. So close that she could almost taste him. She did catch the sweet peppermint scent of his breath. "Liar," he rasped.

No lie. She *was* hot. But the heat she felt had more to do with the sexy Santa before her than with the temperature in the civic center. "You're the one who stopped last night." Like him, she'd dropped her voice. Too many people were around them. Too many voices. Too many eyes watching them. This was a private conversation that she didn't want anyone else to know about.

"If we cross that line, you'll be mine." His fingers tightened around her wrist. "Are you ready to be mine? Is that what you're saying?"

"I—"

"Santa!" Elliott slapped a hand on Brady's shoulder. "Are you getting my sister's Christmas list?" he asked, all jovial and bright even as green paint covered his face. Clearly, the man's heart had multiplied in size throughout the night because his grin stretched from one ear to the other. "Finding out everything she wants?"

I only want Brady. He'd been at the top of Noelle's list for ages. Not like she'd tell her brother that bit of news, however. Her cheeks flushed as her gaze darted between the two men.

"Or maybe," Elliott continued, musingly, "you're telling her what *you* want? I'm sure she'd love to hear what Santa wants. He needs a gift, too, am I right? Not like it's fair for everyone else on the planet to get a present, but Santa winds up out in the cold."

She never wanted Brady to be out in the cold. Never had. Never would. "Santa can tell me what he wants." She cleared her throat. "There's still time to do some shopping," Noelle noted, hoping to get control of the conversation.

Brady's stare remained focused on her. "You already know what I want."

All the moisture seemed to leave her mouth as her heart just galloped away.

Elliott slapped his shoulder again. "Great job, tonight. I could hear your 'Ho, ho, ho' booming across the room." A nod. "Obviously, you have yourself a yearly gig now."

No, he didn't. Because next year, Brady might not even be in Charm for the holidays. He hadn't been in town last Christmas. Instead, he'd been on the other side of the world, and the holiday had felt so lonely even when she'd been surrounded by her family. "I'd hardly say we're booking him for a gig next year. He'll probably be on another mission by then."

Elliott's hand fell away from Brady. "Doubtful, since he's heading for a civilian life."

Her jaw almost hit the floor. "What?"

But her brother didn't seem to hear her question. After a heavy exhale he told Brady,

"Dude, gonna need you to play Santa for about five more minutes. Hate to steal you away from Noelle, but there is one more donor you need to see. Come on." He grabbed Brady's arm.

Brady's mouth tightened. "I'll be right back. We are *not* done," he told Noelle.

"Of course, you're not done." Elliott rolled his eyes. "You're her ride home. Still protecting her, aren't you? I'm counting on you to do your job. Don't let me down."

He led Brady away.

Noelle stood in the middle of the crowd. Brady was done with special ops? No more dangerous missions? No more empty months while he was off the radar? He was home to stay...and he wanted her?

Her hand fluttered as she fanned her flushed face. Damn. It was hot. Too many people. She spun for the door. A breath of fresh air was seriously needed.

***

"Don't let me down," Elliott said again as he pushed Brady toward the room on the right. "I have high hopes, and you had better not screw this shit up." He kicked the door shut with his boot and glared. In his current costume, the glare appeared particularly twisted.

Lifting one eyebrow, Brady glanced around the area. "Where's the donor?"

"There is no other damn donor, but you're in a giant, smelly Santa costume, and you need to change, get your shit together, and go *charm* my sister. You were glaring at her in the middle of the civic center, everyone was whispering, and it sure as hell looked as if the two of you were about to come to blows."

"Definitely not. I would never lay a hand on her, and you know it." He hauled off the Santa coat and shoved it into the box that perched on a nearby table.

"Yeah, well, the way to claim her heart isn't by glaring."

Had he been glaring? He'd felt more like he'd been drinking her in. Every gorgeous inch of her. In that tight Mrs. Claus outfit, she'd been hot enough to make a man drool. Or beg. Maybe both.

"You need to wine and dine her. I know my sister, she's all about charm. And it's the holiday season—she goes crazy for this time of the year. Take her ice skating. Go build a snowman with her. Do something *merry*."

Brady ditched the Santa pants. He'd hauled them on top of his jeans, so now that they were gone and he was just wearing his shirt, jeans, and boots, he could head back to Noelle. Provided, of course, that Elliott got the hell out of his way. "You don't think being Santa was merry?"

"I think she needs more. Ice skating, snowman building, caroling. Those are all things that Noelle likes to do this time of the year."

"I know what she likes," he grumbled. He didn't need lessons on Noelle.

"Sure, you do." Elliott glanced heavenward with a sigh.

Seriously? "*It's a Wonderful Life* is her favorite Christmas movie, and it doesn't matter how many times she watches it, Noelle still cries at the end when Clarence gets his wings and that bell rings."

"Lucky guess." But Elliott's gaze returned to him. "Half the world probably counts that one as their favorite holiday movie."

Fine. "Purple is her favorite color, she only eats pancakes if they have chocolate chips in them, she dreams of having a Pug named Percival just because she thinks that would be *cute,* and she absolutely treasures this old crystal ballerina that she keeps on a shelf in her bedroom."

Elliott sucked in a sharp breath. "How do you know about the ballerina?"

"I know because you broke the thing years ago, and someone had to super glue it back for her." The tips of his fingers had felt weird for days after that incident, thanks to the glue, and he'd thought about decking his buddy more than once back then. "You hit the thing with your hockey stick. You couldn't play hockey for shit, so you shouldn't have been lugging it into her room. And you walked out, and she *cried.*" He hadn't followed Elliott out. He'd stayed with Noelle.

"I..." Elliott dragged a hand over his face. The green paint smudged. "Our grandmother danced. She gave that ballerina to Noelle." A pause. "Gram died the year after she gave it to Noelle, and you're saying...I broke it?" He grimaced. "I don't remember that. Noelle didn't say anything to me about it. Jeez, I feel like crap now."

Why wallow in guilt at this point? "I fixed it. It's fine." It had been fine for years.

Elliott squinted at him. "I played hockey when I was in high school."

"No, correction, you *tried* to play hockey. You did not succeed." He needed to go find Noelle. Since Elliott wasn't getting out of the way, Brady side-stepped around him.

But, with his expression tensing, Elliott moved into his path once again. "She was a *teenager* back then. Younger than us, man. You had better not be saying that you put your damn hands on my sister when she was—"

Oh, *now,* Elliott wanted to take a punch. "I am not saying any such thing. I fixed her ballerina because I never liked to see Noelle sad." Not then, and not now. "For the record, I've kept my hands off her."

Elliott breathed a sigh of relief.

"Until last night," Brady felt duty bound to add. "That changed last night and—"

Elliott's fist plowed into his jaw.

Chapter Six

On the sixth day of Christmas, my true love gave to me...six seconds of being absolutely stunned. Okay, fine, she didn't give me that gift. Her brother did...when he punched me in the face.

—Brady

Brady didn't stagger back. He didn't even flinch. He did squint at Elliott. "What the fuck, man? *Now* you decide to take a swing at me?"

Elliott blinked. Looked down at his fist. "Oh, shit. Sorry. Reflex."

"I thought you wanted me to be with her!"

"I want you to marry her, not, not—" Breaking off, Elliott came in swinging again.

Brady ducked the blows. "You have problems, you know that, right?"

Elliott threw another punch.

Brady locked his fingers around Elliott's fist and stopped the hit. "You've been drinking, haven't you? Someone spiced the eggnog, and you got into it. When you drink, your impulse control goes to negative twenty."

With a jerk, Elliott wrenched his hand free. "You treat my sister with respect!"

"Technically, she kissed me. So I was respecting her. It would have been rude to walk away." Something he'd done before. *Will I ever forget that moment when I left her alone under the mistletoe?* "Not gonna hurt her again," he swore. "If your sister wants to be with me, it's happening. By the way, you'll only get so many free swings before I lose my patience."

Elliott looked down at his feet. His broad shoulders sagged. "I did get into the eggnog."

"I know you did, buddy."

"I was also the one who spiked it."

"I know that, too."

Elliott peeked up at him. "Get me a ride home?"

Brady threw an arm around Elliott's shoulders. Brady was sure he could find a volunteer to drive the guy home. "Someone will love taking your green ass home." He'd take care of Elliott, then Brady could take Noelle home.

Home. Strange, but when he thought of his home...

He always thought of Noelle.

***

Snowflakes tickled her nose. Noelle blew out a slow breath and tilted back her head. The snowfall wasn't heavy. Just light flakes that scattered across the sky. Her body had cooled quickly outside, but every time she thought of Brady...

I am so not over him.

Not over the crush that had started when she was a teen or the far more adult craving that she'd fought for so long. Now, this Christmas, it seemed everything had changed. Brady wanted her, too. So what was she going to do about that?

Not stand out in the cold and shiver her ass off all night, that was for sure, she was—

"*Noelle.*" Hard. Rough.

Her head turned to the right. About ten feet away, standing slightly in the shadows, she saw a man in a Santa suit. Tall, with broad shoulders, and his black gloved hands at his sides.

She smiled. Brady had put the hat and beard back on. "I thought you were getting rid of the costume."

He shook his head. His left hand lifted. He crooked his index finger, indicating that she should come toward him.

The snow fell a little harder as she took a step in his direction. "I didn't hear you come out. Did you finish talking to Elliott?"

Again, he crooked his finger.

Someone was being mysterious. She took a few more steps toward him. The light behind her flickered. She'd gone out the back door of the center, moving onto the patio area behind the main building. No one else was outside, just her and Brady, but she suddenly felt a strange tension fill her body. "We should go inside," Noelle blurted.

His hand fell to his side.

"We need to go home," she added quickly. "Everyone will be clearing out soon, and we don't want to be the last ones here."

"Come...with me." Rough. Grating. Like her name had been.

She didn't step forward anymore. The white beard covered so much of his face, and he'd positioned himself so that he was mostly in the shadows.

I can't see his eyes. Brady's very distinct eyes. "Your voice sounds funny. Hope you're not catching a cold." Because Brady's voice never grated. It rumbled. It rasped. Sometimes, it thundered. But it didn't grate.

He didn't move.

A shiver shook her body. "I'm cold. Let's go back inside." She spun on her heel and started for the French doors.

In a flash, his fingers curled around her shoulders. His grip was hard, painful, and she let out a shocked cry just as—

The doors flew open. Brady stepped outside. Brady, wearing a t-shirt and jeans and frowning as he called, "Noelle?"

She opened her mouth to scream and get his attention, but the man behind her—a man who was *not* Brady—shoved his gloved hand over her mouth even as he used his other arm to wrench her back against him...and he hauled her toward the darkness and shadows.

No, no, no. This couldn't happen! Her hand flew up. She grabbed at the glove over her mouth, and she managed to snag his pinky finger. Noelle yanked that finger as hard as she could and maybe she even heard it snap.

She *definitely* heard her attacker growl, "Bitch!" right before he freed her mouth.

"*Brady!*" Noelle screamed.

His head whipped toward her. Could he even see her in the shadows?

Her attacker's arm tightened around her stomach.

"Noelle!" Brady's voice was a roar as he leapt down the steps and hurtled toward her.

Noelle drove her elbow back into her attacker.

"Fuck." He shoved her forward, and Noelle slipped on the snow-covered ground. She went down, hard, slamming her knees and her palms onto the earth. Behind her, she heard the frantic thud of footsteps rushing away.

"*Noelle!*" Brady dropped to his knees in front of her. His hands flew over her shoulders. Her arms. "Baby, baby, are you all right?"

Her heart pounded hard enough to shake her chest as she looked at him through a curtain of her tousled hair. Her breath sawed in and out, but Noelle nodded. "Fine...I..." She licked her lips. "I thought he was you," Noelle managed to rasp.

Brady pulled her to her feet. Her knees wanted to shake, so she locked them.

"Get inside," Brady ordered. "Now."

"But—"

"I'm getting the bastard." He gently pushed her toward the building. "*Inside.*" Then he ran away, rushing toward the darkness.

Noelle stared after him. A long shiver trembled over her body.

"Noelle?"

Her brother's voice. Her head angled toward him. He'd just stepped outside. Hesitant, Elliott stood near the open doors with the light spilling behind him. "Is everything all right?"

No, no, nothing was all right. Tears filled her eyes, and she hurriedly blinked them away even as she ran toward her brother.

***

Sonofabitch. Rage poured through Brady's veins as he gave chase. He could make out a faint trail of footprints in the snow, and he barreled along that path.

I thought he was you. Noelle's rasping words echoed in his mind and made the rage burn even hotter. When he'd stepped outside, when he'd heard her scream...

Everything inside of him had iced. For one moment, he hadn't even been able to breathe. Then the fury had kicked in, and he'd flown toward her even as that bastard in the Santa suit— Brady had been able to make out the bulky suit even in the darkness—had heaved her forward and onto the ground.

That the SOB had dared to touch her, had scared her, had...*what the fuck was his intention? What had he planned for my Noelle?*

Brady kicked something in the snow. Something that tangled around the top of his boot. Frowning, he bent down, and his fingers closed around a beard. A long, white Santa beard. Jaw locking, he headed forward. After a few feet, he found a discarded coat. A hat. The red Santa pants.

And Brady reached the driveway. The long, curving drive that was filled with cars coming and going to the charity event. He looked to the left. To the right. People were everywhere. Men. Women. Laughing. Talking.

The jerk had ditched the costume. He'd hidden behind it. Now the sonofabitch could be wandering around in plain sight. Brady's hand fisted in the beard. The entrance to the civic center waited to the right. The bastard could have just strolled inside.

To Noelle?

To try and take her again?

Hell, no. That was not going to happen.

***

The police asked questions. So many questions. Elliott had called them. Or maybe Brady had, Noelle wasn't sure. A dull headache beat behind her eyes. Two hours had passed, and nearly everyone else had gone home already.

"You can't describe anything about the individual's face?" This was the same question the blond-haired cop had asked her three times already.

Noelle hunched into her chair. She still wore her costume, and she desperately wanted to change. It had gotten dirty and wet when she fell into the snow. "He was dressed like Santa. I-I...the beard covered his face."

The blond cop and his female partner shared a long look. "But you were outside with him for several moments before he did anything. You were...talking? Talking all that time, and you can't describe him at all?"

She opened her mouth to respond and say that no, they hadn't been chatting it up out there. She'd gone out to get air, to cool down, and he'd been in the darkness.

"Seriously?" Brady stepped forward. He'd been right behind her, a furious, dangerous presence at her back during the questioning. "You're going to grill *her?* Going to act like she did something wrong?"

"Uh, no." The blond's eyes widened. "We were just trying to figure out—"

"Figure out why none of the building's security cameras were operational," Brady cut through the cop's words to order. "Figure out who the hell turned them off. Figure out why this guy has been targeting her. Figure that shit out, would you?"

"Brady." Elliott's voice, like a calm in the middle of one very pissed-off storm. "They're trying."

"*He could have taken her.*" Brady's voice snapped, whip-like.

Noelle flinched.

"I didn't even know he was out there with her," Brady continued, tone thick with fury. "He had her in the dark. He was taking her away from me. I was supposed to keep her safe, and I fucked up."

Her head snapped toward him. "You didn't!" When Brady had come out, she'd—

"You thought he was me."

Yes.

"He knew that. He was counting on that. He drew you close enough so that he could get his hands on you." Brady's blue eyes glittered with fury. His very, very distinct eyes.

"Ahem." The female cop cleared her throat. "If you thought it was ah, Mr. Breckridge, then I can assume the attacker was of a similar height and build?"

She'd told them this stuff already. The repeated questions were not helping anything. "Same rough height. As far as the build, that would be hard to say because of the coat he wore." She forced herself to look away from Brady's intense gaze. "The pinky on his right hand could be broken. I grabbed it and wrenched as hard as I could when Brady came outside because the man..." Fear pulsed in her stomach. "He had one hand around my waist, and the other over my mouth and he was trying to pull me away, and I knew I had to get Brady's attention. So I yanked the jerk's pinky as hard as I could, because when I was fifteen, Brady taught me that trick and I never forgot it. Doesn't matter how big your attacker is..." She could still remember Brady's grim expression as he talked to her so long ago.

"Everyone's pinky breaks the same. You grab it, and you snap. You—"

"Noelle!" Rowen stood just inside the civic center's doorway. A long, black coat swirled around his legs, and flecks of snow dotted his hair. He hurried toward her with his gloved hands outstretched. "I heard about what happened just as I was finishing up dinner! How terrifying! Are you all right?" Lines of concern etched across his forehead.

Before he could touch her, Brady stepped into his path. "Nope."

Rowen stopped. "Excuse me?"

"Where the hell were you tonight?" Brady demanded.

"At dinner. I just told you I was—"

"Who can vouch for you? You got someone who can give you an alibi?" Brady's questions were rapid-fire.

Noelle rose and peeked around Brady's broad shoulder.

Rowen's outstretched hands slowly dropped. "Why?" Then his eyes widened. "You don't seriously think *I* had anything to do with this attack?"

"Alibi," Brady snarled.

Rowen's mouth tightened. His gaze found Noelle. "Addison texted and told me what happened. I was eating with a friend, and, yes, she can vouch for me, but you have to know I would never do anything to hurt you!" He tried to side-step around Brady.

Brady moved with him. "You have trouble with the 'nope' meaning, don't you? Let me help.

Nope, you are not touching her. She's had one hell of a night, and I'm taking her out of here. No one is going to hurt her, and I will do whatever it takes to keep her safe. Count on it."

Elliott's arm bumped into hers. "I don't think our Brady is quite in control." A low murmur, meant for her alone.

She quite agreed with her brother. Tension poured from Brady, and his hands were fisted once again. In all the years she'd known him, Noelle had never seen him quite like this.

"Uh, Mr. Breckridge." The blond cop again. Ryan? She thought that had been his name. "We will investigate this case. You can be assured of that."

"*Three* attacks," Brady gritted out. "He's come for her three times. First at the house she'd planned to show, then he sent the kids to scare her, and now he comes straight for her in the dark. We don't know what the fuck he will do next."

Her stomach twisted. She inched closer to her brother.

"He could hurt her," Brady continued as his voice thickened. "He could try to kill her. You think I'm going to let that shit happen? You think I will let anyone ever—"

"*Brady.*" Elliott's voice. Not a murmur any longer. A sharp snap with command.

Brady whirled toward him.

"You're scaring Noelle," Elliott added grimly. He'd wiped most of the green off his face, but stubborn smudges still remained. "Stop it. Just get her out of here, okay? Get her someplace safe, and I'll work to figure out why the hell the cameras weren't operating."

Brady's stare shot to Noelle. "I'm scaring you?" He took a hesitant step toward her. "I-I never want that."

"You don't scare me. You couldn't." He made her feel safe, and she very, very much wanted to get the hell out of there. "Take me out of here? Please?"

"We have a few more questions," Ryan began.

Noelle shook her head. "I've answered them all. Again and again. I don't know who it was. I don't know why he's doing this. I just want it to stop." She extended her hand toward Brady.

His fingers closed around hers. "I've got you."

Warmth spread through her. Warmth that came from where their hands touched, slid up her arm, and thawed the chill from her bones. He tugged her toward the exit, and she could feel the stares on them, but she didn't care. She just wanted out. As soon as they stepped into the night, the cold air swept around her, but Brady still held her hand, and she didn't care about the cold. In moments, they were in his SUV, she was safe in the passenger seat, and they were driving away from the civic center.

She loved this charity night, or, she had loved it. Now, when she thought about the event, Noelle just felt scared. Uncertain. What if—

"I'm sorry." Brady's rough apology. "I let you down."

What if Brady hadn't been there? Would she still have gotten away from her attacker? "You saved me."

"The fuck I did. You saved yourself."

"You distracted him. He eased his hold, and I used the move you taught me." The finger break and the elbow to the ribs. Brady had taught her that, too. "If you'd been another minute later, I..."

The windshield wipers sliced across the snow that had fallen onto the glass in front of them.

"You thought he was me." Grim. Thick.

"He wanted me to think that. He was trying to get me close to him. He crooked his stupid gloved finger and just trusted that I would run to him because I always run to you."

Brady's head jerked toward her. "What?"

She was too tired for this. Adrenaline had fueled her during the questioning scene with the cops, but now, weariness pulled at her. "I always run to you."

"No, no, baby, you don't—"

Her eyes closed. *Why stop now?* "I have been in love with you since I was a teenager. My brother knows it. Most people close to me know it. That jerk out there knows it. He thought all he had to do was pretend to be you, and I'd rush into his arms." She *almost* had. "But there's only one you, and he did not feel right to me."

"Noelle."

She kept her eyes closed. After that big confession, she couldn't face Brady yet. A tear slid down her cheek. "Just get me away from this place? Please?"

The vehicle surged forward. "Baby, I'll do anything you want. Always. Remember that."

Chapter Seven

On the seventh day of Christmas, my true love gave to me...enough nightmares to last me for seven lifetimes. Noelle being taken? Noelle being hurt? My worst fear. Nothing can ever happen to her. I'd be lost without Noelle.

—Brady

"This...isn't my house."

Brady killed the engine and glanced toward Noelle. He thought she'd drifted off to sleep during the drive. A feat he would have deemed impossible considering what she'd been through, but she'd closed her eyes and hadn't opened them. And after her sad plea to get her out of there—her *please* had broken his heart—after that, she hadn't spoken again. Until now.

She was right, of course, this wasn't her house. "I brought you to my cabin." Before he'd learned about the bastard terrorizing her, Brady had planned to spend the holidays in the old cabin. He'd had a team come in and clean up the place, get it ready for winter, and fully stock the cabin with supplies and food. But, of course, once Elliott had told him that Noelle had faced a masked man who'd chased her from a real estate open house, everything had changed for Brady.

"I haven't been here in years." She leaned forward to peek out of the windshield. He'd turned off the wipers already, and snow fell against the glass. "You and Elliott would come here a lot before—" Stopping, Noelle cut a glance his way.

But he finished for her, "Before my parents had a marriage that went to hell and then they both were killed in that crash?"

She swallowed. "Yes."

"Good memories were at this cabin. After my folks died, being here hurt, so I stayed away." Away from the cabin and away from the big house in Charm. He reached for the handle of his door.

Her fingers brushed against his arm. "If it hurts, why are we here now?"

Because Brady didn't care if it hurt him, not as long as she was safe. "He could be watching your house. He got those kids to attack last night. Sure, it seemed like a prank on the surface, but trying to take you tonight was no game. I didn't want him trying something again. So I brought you here, where you'd be safe."

Her fingers fell away. "He could have followed us." A whisper of fear slid beneath the words.

"No." Of this, Brady was certain. "The roads up this mountain are dangerous, curving like hell. He would have needed his headlights, and I checked in my rearview. No one followed us." He wanted her to understand this. "You are safe. You can go inside and crash and not have to worry about anything all night long." She needed that reassurance.

Safety. He would give her that. Hell, if Noelle wanted, he would give her everything.

When he pushed open the door, frigid air immediately swept into the SUV. He jumped out and rushed around to her side, but Noelle had already stepped out. "You don't have on a coat," he groused. Reaching into the back seat, Brady grabbed his coat and slid it around her shoulders. The big coat seemed to swallow her whole.

They took a few steps forward, and she slid, falling off balance on the frozen ground. Her hand flew out to grab him. "Elf shoes," she mumbled with a shake of her head. "Not the smartest for snow. Sure, they looked cute but—*Brady!*"

He'd scooped her into his arms. "I've got you." No way was she falling on his watch. He carried her through the snow and up to the cabin. Her arm slid around his neck when he unlocked the door and carrying her across the threshold seemed like the most natural thing in the world to him.

It's not. Get a grip, man. You're not some husband carrying his beautiful bride. She's scared and cold and you need to be a freaking gentleman. He kicked the door shut behind him. It was warmer in the cabin than it had been outside, but not by much. Dammit. "Give me a second to get the heat going." He'd turn on the heater and light the fireplace. No way would Noelle be cold for long. Carefully, he lowered her until Noelle's shoes touched the floor. Her hand lingered around his neck. "I'll be right back." He pulled away. Secured the door. Rushed for the heater. Brady cranked up the temp so that she would be warm, and a few moments later, he had the fire flaring to life in the den.

As he stoked the fire, he heard the rustle of clothing behind him. Figuring that Noelle must be ditching the coat he'd given her, he turned around and...

Not ditching the coat. Well, yes, she was. The coat hung off a nearby chair. But she'd also tossed her red sweater onto the chair. Obviously, Noelle believed in matching because a sexy red bra cupped her breasts and boosted them ever so beautifully.

"Wh-what are you doing?" Yes, his voice came out as half strangled.

She quirked one brow at him. He'd hit the lights earlier so there was plenty of illumination that allowed him to see her. Every delectable inch of her. "Ditching my dirty clothes." Her hands went behind her back and seemed to lower toward her hips. *Her skirt.*

The hiss of a zipper filled the air.

His dick—already saluting her with a major standing ovation—jerked eagerly. "Noelle..."

The skirt fell down her legs. She still wore her tights. Red tights that matched just like everything else. The elf shoes had been kicked away.

He waited for her to take off more. *Please, God, yes, take off more.* The bra. The tights. The panties that she probably had beneath the tights. She could just take them all off. Get rid of everything.

"I hid from you on the way home," Noelle confessed.

Uh, no, she'd been right next to him.

"I was embarrassed because I said something I shouldn't have."

Brady took a lurching step toward her. "You don't ever need to be embarrassed around me." Fucking *never*. As for what she'd said, "Noelle, listen, I need to tell you—"

Her chin lifted. "You told me before...back at my house, you said you wanted to strip me."

Hell, yes. She was partially stripped right then. Too tempting. Too gorgeous. And if she could just take off a little more, she'd make him the happiest bastard in the world.

But she didn't take off more. She sucked in a deep breath and added, "At my house, you said you wanted to fuck me."

Nothing would satisfy him more. Driving into her, sinking into heaven. Having his dream in his arms...*yes.*

"And...y-you said you wanted me to scream your name until I went hoarse."

The faint stutter in her voice had his heart aching. "You always did have one hell of a memory." Say something to Noelle once, and she'd remember it forever. A fact he'd tucked away in his Everything-About-Noelle mental file years ago.

"I would like all of that." A hesitant nod. "Especially tonight. Screaming and being with you and *not* thinking about him or how close he was or what might have happened if you hadn't come out when you did."

He leapt for her. Couldn't stay away. Brady closed the distance between them and curled his hands around her waist. "I'm sorry."

She blinked those incredible eyes of hers at him. So deep. Enchanting. The kind of eyes that owned a man, body and soul. "For what?"

"For letting you go." *For wasting so much time.* "I should have been with you." Not just that night, but always.

"You were changing out of your costume. I just stepped outside for air." A broken laugh. "The attack was hardly something you could predict."

No, she didn't understand. "*I should have been with you,*" Brady said again. What he meant was that instead of running, instead of thinking that he could let her go, that he would actually be able to keep his sanity if she wound up with some other lucky SOB, Brady should have spent his days and nights with her.

Now the idea of giving her up? Letting some bastard have a life with Noelle while Brady had to walk away? *Not gonna happen.* One hand rose. Brushed back her hair. His other hand stayed curled carefully around her waist. "I'll be between you and any threat." She needed to understand this. Understand *him*. "I will do anything to keep you safe. He comes at you again, and he's a dead man."

A quick inhale. "Brady, that's not—you don't mean that!"

"I mean you are the one person in the world who matters most to me. I've done a shit job of making you realize that fact. Truth be told, *that* was my plan. For you not to know. Because you deserve better than me. I knew it years ago. I know it now." A shake of his head. "Knowing doesn't change anything. I can't let you go again. I *won't*. And if he tries to hurt you..." *I will end him*. Done. "There is nothing I would not do for you."

Her gaze searched his. "I don't want you to kill anyone for me."

Of course, she wouldn't. Not Noelle with her soft heart. But sometimes, dark deeds had to be done. He was the man to do those deeds. He'd spent years doing them.

"I just want you," she whispered. Her hand slid up and pressed to his chest. Right over his heart. The heart that had been hers all along, Noelle just hadn't known it. "I want to scream," she added huskily. "I want to let go. I want to see if all the fantasies I've had in my head about the two of us can come anywhere close to matching reality."

Was she trying to bring him to his knees? Because he was close to falling before her.

"I don't want to be afraid. I don't want to think of him." Noelle swallowed. Her gaze never left his. "I just want to know only you. Everything else can fade away."

Right. Like he was going to deny her. *Never.* "That wonderful memory of yours..." His voice came out ragged and rough. "You remember what else I said at your place, don't you?" He knew she did, but, deliberately, Brady added, "When I have you, you're mine." *I will never give you up.* When you had wanted someone for so long, there would be no going back.

"Of course, I remember that part." A faint smile tilted her lips. "But that means you'll be mine, too, Brady."

"Baby, I always have been." His head lowered, and his mouth took hers.

Chapter Eight

On the eighth day of Christmas, my true love gave to me...at least eight years of longing...eight years of need...all erupting into one incredible night. Fantasies are never supposed to match reality. But with Brady? Reality is even better.

—Noelle

This was happening.

She trembled against Brady, and the tremble had nothing to do with cold or fear. Nope, that tremble came from pure, unadulterated lust. He kissed her with skill, with passion, with enough need to make her quake—and, ah, thus the tremble.

They were in front of a blazing fire. His hand had just slid closer to her ass, and she was half naked in front of him. Maybe she'd had a fantasy like this before, though she hadn't exactly been ditching a dirty Mrs. Claus outfit in said fantasy.

"Tell me if I scare you," he rumbled against her mouth.

Scare her? Ha. Not likely. "How fast can you get out of your clothes?" She curled her hand around his neck and held on tightly.

A laugh slipped from him. Warm and rich and so very Brady. "Not the question I have," he returned.

"No?"

His mouth hovered over hers. Noelle wanted it back on hers.

"How fast can I get you out of *your* remaining clothes?" he growled.

"Should be easy enough," she informed him even as she felt her cheeks flushing. "Push down my tights and panties, and you're basically there."

His body stiffened. Every muscle seemed to go rock hard.

Then he was lifting her up, carrying her to the couch, and even as he lowered her onto the thick cushions, he caught the waistband of her tights. He yanked them—and her panties—down her legs and tossed them to the floor, leaving her on that couch in just her red bra.

For a moment, she had the crazy impulse to try and cover up. Shy, hesitant, too nervous, but then she got a look at his expression. Savage need hardened his handsome face. So much need. All for her. "Brady?"

"The bra has to go." Even as he said those words, his fingers slid under her back. He unhooked the bra and jerked it away from her.

With a flick of his hand, he tossed the bra over his shoulder. Neither one of them looked to see where it landed.

Completely naked on the couch, Noelle peered up at him. *Touch me.* She wanted his hands on her, but he was just staring at her. The moments ticked past. "Uh, Brady?"

"You are fucking perfect."

He still wasn't touching her.

"Not a dream," he rasped.

"God, I hope not," she returned. "I'm tired of those. I want reality."

If he wasn't going to touch her, then she'd take the lead. Her hand went to his waistband. Slid down and touched the hard, thrusting length of his cock behind the denim.

"Baby..." So much lust filled that growled word.

So she stroked him again and then—

Then he moved *fast*. Brady settled between her legs. He shoved half the cushions and pillows off the oversized couch, and he spread her legs so that he could angle in better, and he put his mouth on her.

She'd thought he'd *touch* her. Maybe caress her with those wonderfully wicked, broad fingers of his. But, no, he was tasting. His tongue slid over her clit, and she nearly jumped right off the couch. "Brady!" Her hands flew down and sank into the thickness of his dark hair.

His head lifted. "Want me to stop?"

Hell, no. "No," she breathed.

"Good." His mouth went back to her. Licking. Kissing. And his fingers joined his lips and tongue.

Her hips rose to meet him, and her eyes pretty much rolled back into her head because what he was doing felt incredible. Maybe it should have been awkward. Maybe she should have been reserved, but the hesitancy she'd felt before had vanished. This was Brady. She'd wanted him forever, and he was—she was...

His tongue thrust into her. His fingers rubbed over her clit. She came, a fast, hard explosion of release that rocked her whole body. She called out his name, a breathless cry, not a scream because she didn't have the breath for a scream. She was too busy riding her release, feeling it pulse through her entire body and knowing that this was just the start.

Brady.

"Delicious. Just like I knew you would be." He pushed up, slowly. Brady licked his lower lip and his eyes seemed to burn even brighter.

Aftershocks had her twisting beneath him. "Brady, I want you inside of me."

"There's no other place I want to be." But he rose from the couch. Left her.

"Brady?"

Holding her gaze, he yanked his shirt over his head. Tossed it so it joined her clothes. He kicked out of his boots, ditched his socks, and his jeans fell to the floor—but not before he took something from his wallet.

Condom.

The man had come prepared.

While she watched him, he rolled the condom on his dick. His very, very large dick. She sat up. "Uh, Brady, we should..." Noelle stopped because she wasn't sure what to say. *We should go slowly because you look really big.* Nope, not that. *You're bigger than the guys I've had before.* Again, no, though those words would probably go straight to his head.

His fingers teased her nipple. He'd reached out to touch her, and, already sensitive, she gasped at the contact. Her hair slid down and brushed over his wrist.

"Your breasts are beautiful. You are beautiful. And, baby, if I don't get inside of you, I'll lose my mind."

She caught his wrist. Lifted the hand that had been stroking her. "We can't have that." She brought his hand to her mouth with a whole lot more confidence than she actually felt, but she was trying to at least *appear* confident. Trying not to show the stupid nerves that had just come flooding back. She parted her lips, and, watching him, she slid his index finger into her mouth. She sucked his finger.

The blue of his eyes brightened even more.

"Noelle." And that was it. A possessive growl of her name. Then he scooped her up. Lifted her into his arms again, like holding her weight was the easiest thing in the world. Spoiler, she knew it wasn't. Brady was just incredibly strong. Noelle thought he was going to carry her somewhere—maybe a bedroom with a nice, lush bed—but, instead, he turned and took a few fast steps toward a nearby doorway.

"Wrap your legs around me," he ordered.

She did.

"Look the fuck up," he said.

What?

But she looked up. She looked the fuck up and saw mistletoe. Her breath shuddered out. "Why...?"

"I wanted you here. Wanted another chance. Wanted that kiss I missed so long ago." Each word seemed torn from him, ragged with desire. "Wanted...you."

Her gaze flew back to him. "You have me."

His mouth took hers as he thrust into her. Slow, deep, inch by thick inch, Brady filled her. A moan broke from her, and her legs tightened even more around him. He didn't stop, not until he had filled her completely.

And then...

Then the madness began. A storm seemed to break inside of her. Need, desire that she'd held back too long flooded through her. Suddenly, she wasn't just holding him. Her nails clawed at Brady as she fought to pull him ever nearer. He withdrew. Thrust deeper. His hands were hot brands around her hips as he lifted her up and down. He took a step to the side. Another. Brady had positioned her now so her back pressed to the wall. Deeper, harder, his thrusts had her becoming even wetter. Even wilder.

He tore his mouth from hers and kissed a fiery path down her neck. She squeezed him with her inner muscles as tightly as she could.

"Fucking heaven," he growled.

He withdrew. Plunged in deeper. Drove her straight into her orgasm as she screamed his name.

"*Yes, yes.*" He kept thrusting. "You feel too good. *Better than any fantasy.*"

She could barely hear him over the drumbeat of her heart. Pleasure pulsed through every cell of her body, and Noelle just wanted to go limp and let the release consume her.

"*Noelle.*" He stiffened. Surged into her once more and...

Her eyes opened. She saw the fierce pleasure lash across his face as he came. A release that just fed her own as the climax rolled through her on an endless wave. She'd never felt so close to anyone in her life. Bonded. Linked, body and soul.

He was hers. Completely and totally in that moment. And it really only seemed fair since she had belonged to him for a very, very long time.

She'd given him her heart years ago. He just hadn't known it. Since then, no one else had ever been able to truly get close to her. How could they? No other man could compete.

Not when she had been in love with Brady all that time.

***

He carried her to the bedroom and tucked her under the thick covers because he didn't want Noelle getting cold. Brady ditched the condom, hauled on a pair of old sweats, and was on his way to join Noelle in that cozy bed when his phone rang.

He stopped halfway to the bed. Noelle's eyes remained closed. *Asleep already?*

The phone rang again. Cursing softly, he spun on his heel and marched to the den. Their clothes littered the floor, but he scrounged around until he snagged his phone. Elliott's smiling picture filled the screen. Wincing—because yep, no way did Elliott need to know what Brady had been doing five minutes ago—he took the call and put the phone to his ear. "She's safe and sound, sleeping in my bed."

Silence.

Shit. Okay, he probably should not have added the "my bed" part to that sentence. He should have just stopped after the "sound" bit.

Brady cleared his throat. "I took her to my cabin, not her place. I was worried the jerk might try something there. I needed to get her away." *And all to myself.* Yes, selfish, but true. He'd wanted her far away from everyone else and far from any other threat out there.

"I want this bastard stopped, Brady." Elliott's voice was devoid of its normal humor. Most folks thought Elliott was easy going, the fun one to be around. Elliott always had people smiling and laughing while Brady was the intense and dark one.

Folks thought wrong. Elliott's quick grin was a lie. Beneath the surface, he was just as intense and dark as Brady. One of the reasons why they were such good friends. "You and me both."

"He could have kidnapped her tonight. He could have fucking *hurt* her. He could have—" Elliott broke off.

A good thing. Brady didn't need a list of all the things that could have happened. He already knew. The fears kept playing through his mind on repeat. "He knows her," Brady said as he cast a quick glance over his shoulder to make sure that Noelle was still sleeping. "He's someone in her life. Someone close enough that he knew she'd be going to that real estate listing when he first scared the hell out of her."

"Anyone could have known that," Elliott threw back. "It was an open house, listed on our company website. Not some big secret."

True enough, and her home address would certainly be something easy enough to obtain, but the part that told him this was someone close to her... "The Santa suit."

"What?"

"The charity event is personal for her. He waited until she was on her own, and the SOB came with his own freaking Santa suit so he'd be disguised. Hell, she said he crooked his finger and beckoned her closer. He wanted her to think he was me. I think the bastard knows about my relationship with her." *Relationship.* "He knows I was at her place last night. He thought she'd rush to him—*because she thought he was me*—and that he could get her away without any problem."

"The prick needs to think again."

"He won't stop. He's not just going to turn away and give up." Brady believed this to his core. "I'm not letting her out of my sight. Until we have the bastard, where she goes, I go."

"And that's why she's in your cabin? So you keep her in your sight?"

He took a few steps back, turned and looked into the bedroom. He'd left the door open so he could see her. In the bed, she still slept. "I would kill for her without any hesitation."

"I know." Gruff. "So the hell would I."

Yes, Elliott would. But he had no experience with killing. Brady did. "I won't lower my guard. Neither will she." A pause as he drank in the sight of Noelle. Voice low, he asked, "What did you find out about the security footage?"

"No one knows why the cameras shut off. The guard on duty said he actually caught a couple making out in the security room a bit before everything happened with Noelle. The cops questioned the couple, but they swear they didn't see anyone."

Alarm bells blasted in Brady's mind. "Who was the couple?"

"Addison Lane and her date, Trevor McIntosh."

He didn't remember seeing Addison with a date. When she'd approached him and Noelle, it had just been her. "Addison doesn't like your sister."

"She's in competition with my sister," Elliott corrected. "I'm pretty sure she views Noelle as her biggest competition in town."

"And you're not competition?"

"I'm in the background. It's Noelle that everyone loves at our company. She's got the biggest client listing of any agent in the county."

Of course, she did. With her quick smile and sharp mind, you had a friendly shark on your side when you wanted to make a real estate deal. "What do you know about the Trevor guy?"

"He's the mayor's nephew. Just in town for the holidays. I think he's a med student at Emory. Poor guy is gonna be in over his head with Addison. She'll eat him for breakfast."

There was something about Elliott's voice. A little too much certainty and personal knowledge. "You were involved with Addison."

"Briefly. Very, very briefly. Two weeks in, and the woman started talking about all the things she planned to do with the real estate company—the company that belongs to me and Noelle. I knew I was being used and can't say that I was exactly fond of Addison's long-term plans for a company that *wasn't* hers and never would be, so we parted ways." A long sigh. "Have to say, though, she seemed really concerned about Noelle tonight. She even called to say she wished that she'd seen something when she and Trevor were in the security room."

"Convenient." Too convenient.

"What?"

"How do we know Addison didn't sabotage the system?"

"Uh, why would she do that?" A quick, confused return from Elliott.

Why, indeed.

"It was a man in the Santa suit," Elliott said. "A man, not Addison."

Yes, Brady hadn't forgotten that part.

"Addison is all of five-foot-five. You would have known if it was her."

"And just how big is this Trevor friend of hers?"

"I—" Elliott stopped. Cleared his throat. "He's about your size."

Brady's hold tightened on the phone.

"But, no, man, you're wrong about this!" Elliott rushed to add. "Addison was with him when that prick in the Santa suit tried to grab Chloe."

"And you know this because...?"

"Because Addison told me," he muttered. "Or, rather, she told the cops. Addison and Trevor are each other's alibis."

How wonderful for them. "I'll be having a chat with those two tomorrow." Hell, yes, he would. Because from where he was standing, Addison and her friend didn't exactly look like the picture of innocence. No, they appeared suspicious as hell.

After a few more minutes of talking with Elliott, Brady hung up the phone. He checked the perimeter, saw nothing but snow surrounding the cabin, and he turned off all the lights. As he walked toward his bedroom, he glanced up at the mistletoe. His jaw hardened. He didn't have any other decorations at the cabin. He'd thought maybe Noelle could help him with that. She could always light up a house.

She lights up my place just by being in it.

But he had requested the mistletoe when he'd ordered the cabin prepared. Why? Because he requested it every year. Because every single year he thought...*Maybe I'll have another chance with*

Noelle. Maybe I can get Noelle here. Maybe I can tell her…

That I love her.

Step one of that master plan had been completed. He had her in the cabin. He had *her*. Now, to just give her the confession he'd kept secret for far too long.

But when he went back into the bedroom, Noelle was still sleeping. She'd curled up on her side, and her hand rested beneath her cheek. For a moment, he just stared at her.

So beautiful.

Swallowing, he reached over and turned off the lamp. He ditched the sweats, slid into bed beside her, and Noelle instantly rolled closer. Her hand reached out and pressed over his heart.

And his arm curled around her to hold her tight.

He stared up at the darkness. Thought about the events of the night. The fear that had chilled him to the bone when she'd screamed. The rage that had erupted as he gave chase after the bastard who'd tried to take her. The savage satisfaction he'd felt when he finally—*finally*—claimed Noelle.

He'd told her brother the truth. Brady would kill in an instant if Noelle was in danger. He would lie, cheat, fight, *destroy* for her. But the one thing he would not do? That he could not do any longer?

Walk away. Give her up.

She was his, and there was no going back.

Chapter Nine

On the ninth day of Christmas, my true love gave to me...a night I will never forget. A nice start. Now I want forever.

—Brady

Her hands slid over his chest. A light, careful caress. Her fingers edged downward, slowly, tentatively, moving down to—

Brady's eyes flew open and found darkness waiting. His hand flew out and curled around Noelle's delicate wrist before she could reach the ever-so-eager part of his body that was already thrusting toward her. "In the mood to play, are you?" he rumbled as the last vestiges of sleep vanished from his mind.

"I was..." She cleared her throat. "I like to touch you."

He let go of her wrist. "Then touch away." Like he'd refuse her anything. And if she wanted to touch him, he'd hold onto his control while she did. Maybe. It just depended on exactly where she was doing her touching.

She reached for his dick.

His teeth snapped together. *Sonofabitch*.

"I had a bad dream," Noelle confessed as her silken fingers danced over the head of his cock. "But then I woke up and you were here."

"I'll always be here." A promise. No more missions. No more leaving his heart behind and fearing that she'd have a ring on her finger when he got back. If she had a ring, it would be his.

"Until duty calls again," she said, voice sad. "But that's the way it is. Can't change things."

No, no, duty wasn't calling again. He was staying with her. He would build a life with her. Brady opened his mouth to tell Noelle that she was his world, that nothing else mattered but...

Her mouth closed around the head of his cock. And speech? Impossible. Brady's hands flew out and fisted in the sheets near him as his hips surged up toward her.

Her tongue licked against him. Her lips parted more. She pulled him in deeper. Sucked with sensual force.

He was a goner. Just done. Like he was supposed to maintain control when the gorgeous source of his obsession was going down on him. Not happening. With a savage growl, he let go of the sheets and grabbed her. Brady pulled her up with gentle force because he wasn't coming in her mouth. He was going to be buried in her core when he came.

"But, Brady, I wanted to—"

He rolled her beneath him. Spread her thighs and pushed right against her. Wet. Hot. *Mine.* The head of his cock shoved against her.

"Condom," Noelle gasped. "We need a condom unless you want a little mini-Noelle with us next Christmas."

That vision—that insanely perfect vision—broke him. He did want that. He wanted a mini-Noelle. He wanted her, a family, laughter, and love. Everything with her—he wanted it, and he would take it. But first...

Put a ring on her finger.

He grabbed for the nightstand. Snagged a condom that was tucked inside. He ripped that thing open and rolled it on in record time. Then he lodged his cock at the entrance to her body.

And sank as deep as he could go in one long, hard thrust.

They both gasped. He felt the slight resistance of her inner muscles and could have kicked his own ass. "Baby, am I hurting you?"

She arched against him. "Do not dare stop now!" A demand. "Move, Brady. Fast and hard. Give me everything."

Everything. That was what he wanted her to give him, so he would gladly give her the same in return. The bed shook beneath his thrusts. Her hands flew frantically over him. He grabbed her legs and lifted them over his shoulders so he could go even deeper. Harder. She urged him on with her breathless cries. So tight and hot and perfect.

The best sex of his life. And for the rest of his life, he knew he'd only want her.

Noelle.

His Noelle.

She tipped back her head and cried out his name. He felt the soft, inner contractions of her muscles and knew she was coming for him. Faster, rougher, stronger, he pounded into her until he found his own body-quaking release. A release that had him holding her with too much force, but he couldn't let go.

Not now that he had Noelle. Too much time had been wasted. Too many years lost. There would be no going back. There would only be... "Marry me," he blurted even as his heart thundered in his chest.

"What?"

He was still inside of her. Still feeling pleasure dance through every nerve in his body. "You said you loved me."

"I—"

"Marry me."

"Are you..." Her head moved against the pillow. He needed to see her eyes. Her face. "Are you serious right now?" Noelle asked with a gasp.

He withdrew from her, and absolutely hated that separation. If he had his way, he'd spend the whole holiday season inside of her.

But he needed to do this right. Or, hell, it was probably too late for right. He'd do it better. "Hold the thought."

"Hold the—" She broke off.

He marched to the bathroom and ditched the condom. On the way back to her, he snagged his sweats. The light from the bedside lamp spilled onto the bed. She'd turned it on when he went into the bathroom. With sheets wrapped around her, Noelle perched on the edge of the mattress and watched him with her deep and wary gaze.

He headed straight for her and dropped to his knees.

Noelle shook her head. "I was afraid this would happen."

He reached for her hand. Threaded his fingers with hers. "Afraid?" That wasn't what he wanted. "You never need to be afraid with me."

"It's because we had sex. You think that because you're friends with my brother that now you have to pull some noble BS and propose." She tugged her hand, trying to pull it back from him even as she shook her head. "The offer is appreciated. Noted. But no thanks."

No thanks. His heart turned to lead. "This has nothing to do with your brother."

"Sex can just be sex, Brady. You don't have to throw a marriage proposal in just because you feel guilty." She swallowed. Blinked away what had better *not* be tears.

He brought their joined hands to his mouth. Pressed a kiss to her knuckles. "I don't feel guilty, and with you, it will *never* be just sex."

"No?" Another click as she swallowed. "Then what will it be?"

"You said you loved me," he reminded her. When they'd been in his SUV, those words had pierced straight to his core. "That you'd been in love with me for years." She couldn't take those words back. Could not. Oh, what the hell would he do if she *did* take them back? Brady realized he was holding his breath.

"Yes." She stared straight at him. "I said that."

A smile stretched over his face. "That's good. So good."

She kept staring at him. No smile curved her lips.

"It's good because I'm completely yours, Noelle. I am in love with you."

A hard shake of her head. "No, you're not. If you were in love with me, you would have said something sooner." She tugged harder and this time, he let her go. He let go because there was pain in her voice. "You feel guilty because we had sex."

"I feel *thrilled* that we had sex. And I want to have sex with you over and over again, and one day, I'd love to have that mini-Noelle you mentioned scampering around a Christmas tree. I. Love. You."

Another shake of her head. "You never said *any* of this before!"

"Neither did you, sweetheart." Not until hours ago.

A tear slid down her cheek. "Why now?"

He hated that tear. His fingers cupped her cheek so he could catch the tear drop. "Because you didn't pick someone else."

"I have no idea what that means!"

"You deserve better than me. I knew it. Always did. But I can be better," he rushed to say. "I'll be careful with you, I swear it. I will make you happy. We can have a good life. I won't ever be like—" His lips clamped together to hold back the words.

Too late.

They both knew who he meant.

And now she reached for his hand. She curled her fingers around his. "You are not your father."

Wasn't that something he'd feared when he was younger? But now he knew. *I'm not.* "The wreck was his fault. They were fighting, as they always did at the end. People saw them fighting before they even got into the car. He drove off too fast. Too angry." Dammit. "He lost control of the car. He always said he loved her, but he hurt her." *He killed her.* The fight—it had been because his mother found out his father had cheated on her. Anger and pain had taken over for them both. And in the end...

I was left with nothing.

No, not true. He'd been left with his best friend and with sweet Noelle. Noelle who had glared at anyone who tried to whisper or gossip. Noelle who had always stood by him. "I would never cheat on you. Hell, I can't even look at other women. You are it for me. You've owned my heart for years. And when we were under the mistletoe together that first time, I wanted to kiss you, but, baby, you were eighteen. You needed a chance to explore the world without me. To live without me. You needed to find your own joy and you needed—"

"I need you." She slipped from the bed. Went to her knees before him. "I need you. I love you. I am not worried that you're like your father. I'm not like my parents. None of us are. We are our own people." Now a smile curled her lips. "Can't even look at other women, huh?"

"Why bother? They aren't you."

Her lips trembled before she threw her arms around him. "And no other man has been you."

His arms curled around her. "Is that...yes?"

"Yes. It's a yes. Most definitely a yes." She pulled back. Beamed at him. "Yes."

Happiness filled him. It lit up all the cold, dark places inside. No, she lit them up. "I fucking love you."

"Say it again."

"*I fucking love you.*"

"I love it when you talk dirty." Her mouth crashed onto his.

He was laughing and kissing her, and they tumbled back onto the floor. She sprawled over him, the sheets tangled between their bodies, and he couldn't believe how lucky he was. He had everything he wanted. Noelle loved *him*. She was going to marry him. They were going to have a life together. He would give her the world.

Everything was so perfect.

Except for the stalker after her. But I'll take care of him.

She lifted her head. Smiled down at him. "We don't even need mistletoe any longer."

No, they didn't. As long as he had Noelle, Brady didn't need anything else. His hand sank into her hair, and he kissed her again.

***

That night, Brady thought they were safe. He thought they'd left the danger back in Charm. He kept on being all blissful and living in denial...right up until the next morning when he went outside and found all four of his tires slashed.

Chapter Ten

*On the tenth day of Christmas, my true love
gave to me...terror. That's it. Pure terror. Ten
minutes—ten years. Felt the same. Because the
bastard hunted us down and came to my cabin.
All I could think about was keeping Noelle safe.*

—Brady

"Go back inside, Noelle," Brady directed as he
stared at the slashed tires.

"Brady?" She'd been right behind him,
holding his hand as they headed out.

He turned a little, making sure to shield her
with his body. He'd searched the snow and didn't
see any tracks, but the woods were only about
twenty feet away. The SOB could be hiding there,
watching.

Worry filled her eyes. "Is he still here?"

Odds were good that the bastard was, yes, and he'd just made sure that they couldn't get away. "I need to search the area." The guy must have a vehicle stashed fairly close by. He'd hidden the ride, then stalked over to slash the tires.

You want us trapped here?

"That's a yes," Noelle whispered. "You think he's here."

A quick nod. "Go in, lock the door, and keep it locked until I come back." He already had on his holster, and his weapon was a solid weight on his side. The bastard had been clever the night before. He hadn't triggered any alarms. His attack had been silent.

"Call the police," he told her. "Get them out here." But it would take time for them to arrive, and if the cops came in with sirens blazing, his prey would run.

That's why I have to get him first.

Noelle nodded but she didn't go inside. "I get that you're the one with the special ops training and all of that, but you be careful, understand me? Because if *anything* happens to you, I will be seriously pissed."

"Nothing will happen." Nothing would come between them.

With one last look, she hurried away and went up the steps that led to the cabin. She already had her phone out, and he could hear her talking to the dispatcher.

He turned back to look at the trees. No tracks at all in the snow. He was pretty sure that the snow had stopped falling about three hours ago. The perp could be long gone by now or...

Or he's waiting. Because, after all, that was what the bastard liked to do.

The first time he'd come after Noelle, he'd been waiting in the open house for her. Just waiting inside for her to come to him.

Then, last night, he'd waited outside the civic center, biding his time until he could get Noelle to come to him once more.

And now he was—

Sonofabitch. Brady whirled back toward the cabin. But Noelle had already disappeared inside. "Noelle!" Brady roared. He didn't rush for the line of trees. Instead, he rushed back for the cabin.

Back for her. Because Brady feared the perp was up to his old tricks again.

He was waiting for Noelle. Waiting inside...

***

"Yes, yes, can you hear me?" Noelle demanded as she pressed her phone to her ear and peeked out the window to try and see Brady. "I need the police." The connection was crap at the cabin. "The address is—"

"Hang up." Low. Grating.

Her breath choked out. "The address is 52 Winter Way—*ah!*"

He ripped the phone from her hand and threw it across the room. She slammed her left hand into the glass of the window, hoping to attract Brady's attention, but even as her fist connected, she was being whipped around to face the man who'd been waiting inside the cabin for her.

A man who wore a ski mask again. A big, bulky coat. And black gloves on his hands.

"You're coming with me," he told her. "We're getting the hell out of here."

That voice...she blinked quickly, and her lips parted as she gazed through the holes in the ski mask and saw his eyes. *Hazel eyes.* Eyes that she knew.

"Rowen?" Noelle shook her head. "What are you doing? I'm not going *anywhere* with you." Rowen was the one who'd been terrorizing her?

"Yes, you are," he snarled right back. "I'm the hero."

Uh, nope. Clearly, he was not.

One of his hands had clenched around her right shoulder, and he held her trapped between his body and the cold panes of the window.

"You wanted me to save you."

Noelle shook her head. "I think you're confused."

"She told me! You've wanted me from the beginning!" With his free hand, he yanked off the ski mask. His usual, perfectly-styled hair shot up in a dozen directions. He dropped the ski mask to the floor. "You want me." Certainty. "We're leaving. We're going to be together."

Her heart thundered in her chest. "I'm with Brady. He's right outside. You need to get out of here before he comes in and finds you." *You need to get the hell out of here now.*

"Brady is nothing! She told me—told me that he'd rejected you years ago." A smile curled his lips. "I won't do that. I won't ever turn you down. Don't you see? I've done all of this for you."

"You've been terrifying me...as a courtship?" Just so she was clear.

"You wanted a hero. You wanted someone to save you. Here I am."

"Heroes don't usually wear ski masks and break into someone's cabin."

His brow furrowed. "I wanted to get close to you. You *wanted* me close, too. I know the signs."

Again, she shook her head. "Whatever you think is happening—it isn't. I'm involved with Brady." A Brady who could come rushing in at any moment, please. *Any. Moment.*

"No. He rejected you! She told me that he walked away from you years ago. When you introduced us in your office, I acted like I didn't know who he was. But I did." Rowen's jaw hardened. "Brady is your past. I am your future."

Hard no.

"You want me, Noelle. You want someone who will sweep in and save you. So I set the scene for you. I did everything. And you were supposed to turn to *me*. You're not supposed to be in this fucking cabin with him!"

"H-how did you even find the cabin?"

He flashed his warm smile. The smile that reassured so many clients. "I have access to public records. You know that. It's our business to know who owns certain properties." The smile slipped. "When you didn't go home, I just checked to see what else that bastard owned. Easy enough to get the address and drive here."

"And you...you came to slash his tires—"

"Because I'm fucking *pissed!*" His fingers tightened on her shoulders with bruising force.

A gasp tore from her.

"You weren't supposed to get close to him. How many times do I have to say it? He rejected you. He turned away from you. Addison told me how you needed to be pushed to see me. That I had to get you scared so you'd need me, and I did, and now we'll be together, and we can ditch that bastard. He doesn't ever need to be around you again because you have me."

Addison. Her stomach knotted. "I think you've been misled." *I think you are dangerous and unstable, and you need help.* "Let me go and we can talk about this situation—"

"What she means..." Brady growled from behind Rowen, "is take your fucking hands off her now before I beat the hell out of you."

Rowen sucked in a sharp breath. But he didn't let her go. He also didn't turn to face Brady. Instead, Rowen gave her his reassuring smile again. The smile was extra scary when paired with the rage that glinted in his eyes. "It's okay," he said to Noelle softly. "You can tell him the truth. Tell him that you want me. That I'm the one you need."

"You're the one who has been terrorizing her," Brady said. His growling voice was closer because he was closing in. "You're the one who scared her."

"I had to make her see me. Addison said...Noelle was too tied up on the past. I had to shake her free. Had to make her feel alive again. She'd want me—she *does* want me—and I'll save her, and everything will be perfect."

"You aren't saving me," Noelle told him as she lifted her chin. Her hand also rose to curl around the hand that gripped her shoulder. She'd broken the pinky finger on that hand before. She'd go for it again.

"Brady doesn't want you," Rowen said as he leaned in even closer to her, bringing his face right in front of Noelle's. "I do. *I want you, and we will be great together.*"

"No, asshole, you won't," Brady blasted. Even as Noelle grabbed for Rowen's hand—intending to twist or break as many fingers as she could—Brady jerked her attacker back. He threw Rowen toward the couch. "You are going to stay the hell away from her." Brady's gaze swept over her. "Baby, you okay?"

A quick nod.

His eyes narrowed. Chips of blue ice. A cold fury ruled him. This scene was not going to end well for Rowen.

She looked to the right just as Rowen spun to glare at them. "You *left* her!" Spittle flew from his mouth. "I'm here for her. I won't reject her. She's going to be mine!"

"You keep harping on the rejection bullshit. Let me correct you." Brady put his body in front of Noelle's. "She's owned my heart for years. Even when I was an ocean away, she was with me. She is *always* with me. In my mind. In my fucking soul. You don't get to scare her. You don't get to attack her. And you don't get to slash my damn tires!"

A high-pitched cry broke from Rowen as he leapt for Brady. Rowen came flying with his hands outstretched, as if he'd wrap them around Brady's throat.

Noelle screamed and grabbed for the lamp on the nearby table. She'd slam that into Rowen and—

Brady punched him. A fast hit to the jaw that was immediately followed by an upper cut. She actually heard Rowen's teeth snap together before he stumbled back. His body weaved, and Brady hit him again. Twice more. Powerful blows that sent Rowen retreating even more. When he hit the edge of the couch, Rowen fell back, careening over the cushions before finally slamming onto the floor.

Silence.

Tension poured from Brady's body, and she saw his hands clench and unclench. His gaze stayed on Rowen's fallen form. Rowen barely seemed to be breathing.

"Did you call the cops?" Brady asked, voice icy.

"Uh, I was doing just that." She let go of the lamp because clearly it was not going to be needed. From the look of things, Rowen was out cold. Noelle scampered to the left and scooped up her phone. When she looked at it, she realized the call had never disconnected. Putting the phone to her ear, she asked, "Are you still there?"

"*Ma'am! Ma'am!*" The operator's frantic voice cracked in Noelle's ear. "Help is on the way! Can you get in a safe location?"

Noelle moved to Brady's side. Her shoulder brushed against him. "I am in a safe location."

"Good." Relief filled the dispatcher's voice. "Stay there."

She fully intended to stay with Brady. Now. Always.

"Units will be arriving shortly."

Rowen let out a low groan. When he heaved up, Noelle saw blood dripping from his mouth and nose. "You...you..." Rowen mumbled as he pointed at Brady.

"Yes, me." Brady slanted a look at Noelle. "How long until the cops arrive?"

"*Five minutes,*" the dispatcher said into her ear. "Our ETA is five minutes."

"Five minutes," she told Brady, wetting her lips.

"Excellent. Plenty of time for me to teach Rowen that I will always be between him and you." He closed in on his prey. "Ready for the first lesson to begin?"

Rowen tried to headbutt him.

Brady easily dodged the attack. "I'll take that as a yes." He sprang forward.

Rowen *didn't* dodge Brady's attack.

Chapter Eleven

On the eleventh day of Christmas, my true love gave to me...eleven eager cops waiting to make a bust. Yep, because the story is wrapping up and the cops are closing in.

—Noelle

Noelle squared her shoulders, lifted her chin, and knocked lightly on the wooden door before her. The colorful wreath that hung on the door trembled with the vibrations from the knock.

"You sure that you're okay?" Brady murmured from beside her.

Oh, she was more than okay. She was riding a righteous wave of fury.

The door swung open.

Addison Lane frowned at her. "What in the hell?" She tightened the belt of her white, silk robe. "It's ten o'clock on a Saturday morning,

Noelle! Why are you banging on my door?" Her gaze shifted to Brady. Warmed considerably. "Though you can bang me anytime, handsome."

"Save that crap." Disgusted, Noelle shook her head. "I'm here because I know you sent Rowen after me."

Addison's eyes widened, but only for a moment. Quickly, she narrowed them as she shot a dismissive glance over Noelle. "Rowen? What on earth are you talking about?"

"Rowen has been stalking Noelle." Brady's voice was flat. "He was the one dressed in the Santa suit last night. He was the one waiting for her at the open house. And he tried to get her at *my* cabin just hours ago."

Addison rocked back on her heels. "How utterly shocking. Rowen." A shrug. "I guess there is just no understanding what drives some people." Her hand curled around the doorknob. "Don't know why you are coming to tell *me* all of this, though."

"Because you were the one who sent Rowen after me." Noelle maintained her position. Within the pockets of her thick coat, her fingers curled and her nails bit into the palms of her hands. "You told him that if he could play hero, if I were scared and he had to rush in and be the white knight, I'd see him. I'd want to be with him. You told him everything to do."

A brittle laugh escaped Addison. "I'm sure I have no idea what you're rambling about." She yawned. "I need more beauty sleep. Goodbye." Addison swung the door shut.

Correction. She *tried* to swing it shut. Brady put his size fourteen shoe in the way. and the door flew back. "We aren't done," he told her.

Her jaw hardened. "Look, handsome, you're losing your appeal with every moment that passes. How about you get off my porch and go away? Don't you have a war or a mission or something in another country that you need to go handle? Can't you leave again? Immediately?"

"Brady is home to stay," Noelle informed her.

"Well, how wonderful for you." Addison's glare sharpened even more. "Now get the hell away from—"

A siren cut through her words.

Addison paled.

Noelle smiled. "We beat them here, but only by a few minutes. See, Rowen was extremely cooperative with the cops." She pulled her left hand from the coat pocket and curled her fingers around Brady's arm.

"I helped with that cooperation because I'm a good motivator," he admitted modestly.

"Addison, you turned off the security cameras at the charity event." Noelle heard the cars braking behind her, but she didn't look back. "You encouraged Rowen's attacks."

More weak laughter from Addison. "I have no idea what you mean." But her hand trembled when she brushed back a lock of her hair. "And there is certainly nothing wrong with talking to a man. I mean, yes, perhaps I did tell Rowen that he should pursue you." Her gaze darted between Noelle and Brady. "But that was just because I felt sorry for you. You were so alone. Always looking all lost and lovesick. Your brother told me how he worried so much about you. How he could never be settled until you were, so, of course, being the loving person I am, I wanted you to be happy."

A car door slammed.

Addison flinched. "They need to leave. I can't have my neighbors seeing those patrol cars." She craned to look around Brady and Noelle. "There will be so much gossip."

"Oh, there will be plenty of gossip," Noelle promised her. "Because they're taking you in for questioning. See, Rowen didn't just talk about how you encouraged him to terrorize me—"

"Pursue you, I said he should pursue—"

"But he also talked about how the two of you have been helping yourselves to some of the valuables in the houses that you've both listed for sale. You can't steal from clients. You don't get an all-access pass to their jewelry. Just how long have you been taking what you want?"

Addison's mouth dropped open. "He told you? That sonofabitch!" Her voice rose to a shriek. "That was his idea! He said he'd done it before! That just taking a few things here or there wouldn't be noticed! I only—only took a little!" Her words rang clearly for all to hear, and Noelle knew the cops were eager to take in every word. "I can give it back," Addison rushed to say. "This is all a misunderstanding. Just take it!"

Noelle stepped back. So did Brady. After all, they needed to make sure the cops had room to go and grab their suspect. "I'm pretty sure they will take it," she assured Addison. "After they take you in for questioning, it will just be a matter of time before they have a search warrant to go through your house."

The cops closed in.

"Merry Christmas," Noelle told Addison.

Addison screamed.

"And happy new year," Brady added.

***

The minute he had Noelle back in the car—not his SUV, but a rental—Brady cranked up the heat. "Feel better now?" he asked her.

"Yes. Much, much better."

Because he knew she'd wanted to face off with Addison herself. A little Christmas closure could be a great gift.

"They're not going to be hurting anyone else," Brady promised her. The whole tangled story had spilled from Rowen's bleeding lips. That piece of shit sure couldn't take a punch, and, when threatened, he'd been more than happy to spill every secret he had.

Like the fact that he and Addison had been stealing from real estate clients.

Like the fact that Addison had turned off the security cameras at the charity event.

Like the fact that Rowen had lied about his alibi the night of the charity event. There had been no date at the restaurant.

Or like the fact that Addison had big plans for Elliott—she wanted to marry the guy and take over his and Noelle's company.

Only in order to do that, she'd needed Noelle out of the way. Dumbass Rowen had thought that

Addison was trying to hook him up with Noelle, but really, she'd just wanted someone to terrify Noelle into leaving town and clearing her path.

She'd used Rowen.

Rowen had terrorized Noelle.

Now they both would pay.

And Noelle would be safe. Safe, happy, and...*mine*. "You don't need protecting any longer." The threat was over. Even as he watched, Addison tried to make a break and run across the snow-covered yard in her slippers and robe. She didn't get far, though, not before she slipped in the snow and fell on her ass.

The cops formed a circle around her.

"No, I don't." Noelle's quiet response.

His head turned toward her. "I need you," he told her. "I always have. Always will." He didn't think Noelle understood just how much he truly did need her. "You're everything for me."

Her hand rose and pressed to his cheek. "You love me."

"Hell, yes."

"Then take me home, Brady. Let's go home and make love and forget the rest of the world."

His head turned, and he kissed her palm. And then...

He was pretty sure all his tires screeched as he hauled ass out of there.

Noelle laughed softly, and he knew that everything was going to be all right. No, better than all right.

Safe. Happy.

Fucking merry and bright—*that* was what things would be. This holiday was just the start for them. After Christmas, they would have forever waiting.

And forever with Noelle sounded incredible to him.

Chapter Twelve

On the twelfth day of Christmas, my true love gave to me...everything I ever wanted.

—Brady

"The Christmas tree isn't straight. It's leaning too much to the right."

At the critique, Brady locked his hands around the top of the ladder and turned to glower down at his best friend. "It's perfectly straight."

Elliott continued to critically eye the tree. "Nope, definitely leaning to the right." He moved around the ladder and went to the right. "I can help you adjust it, don't worry." He wiggled the tree.

The ornaments shook.

"Stop!" Brady barked.

Elliott raised a brow. "Someone is feeling stressed, are we?" He glanced around the den. "By the way, is it my imagination or did Christmas just vomit in your house?"

"Christmas did not *vomit* in my house." Dammit. Brady climbed down the ladder. "A professional crew just left. A crew that spent hours decorating everything so the place would be perfect." He pulled Elliott's grabby hands away from the tree. "And it's not leaning. It's standing straight and tall." Brady knew because he'd had the team check three times before they left.

"You had a professional crew come in and deck out your house." Elliot nodded. "Because that's something you do now? What's next? Oh, wait, please tell me that you will suddenly be breaking out and singing Christmas carols? I mean, we joked about that shit before, but if you do it for real, I will pay to see that." Laughter tumbled from him.

Smartass. "What's next?" That had been one of Elliott's many questions. "Easy. I get your sister to marry me."

That statement stopped Elliott's laughter. "You're serious?"

"Technically, I have already asked her." Brady exhaled. "But I called you over because you know she'll want your blessing, and I want her happy, so let's just get to that part, can we?" He tried not to appear nervous. "The blessing."

"You decorated for her."

"Well, I damn well didn't do it for myself." He turned to study the tree once more. All fifteen feet of that baby. "We both know she loves this house." The rambling Victorian that had been in his family forever. "I want it to be her home. Our home." A home filled with good memories that would replace all the bad ones. A home that would know laughter and love.

The front door opened. But unlike Elliott, Noelle didn't enter silently. She came rushing inside with a clatter of her heels. The sweet scent of her perfume filled the air as she called out, "Brady? Brady, what's the emergency? I rushed over as soon as I could—*oh*." She stopped just under the curved entrance that led to the den. Her eyes went first to the tree. Then to the mantel that was decked out with festive garland. Then up the mantel to the heavy wreath that hung on the bricks. Her mouth dropped open, and her gaze swung back to him.

"I think he had a decorating emergency," Elliott murmured. "Christmas exploded in here, and he needed you to see it."

"Beautiful," Noelle breathed.

"Yeah," Brady agreed gruffly, unable to take his gaze off her as she stood there in a deep green sweater with a red scarf around her neck. Snowflakes dusted her dark hair. "You are."

She beamed at him. All Brady wanted to do was sweep her into his arms and make love to her right under the lights of the tree. He took a step forward.

Elliott tapped his shoulder.

Right. He was still there.

"How much do you love my sister?" Elliott asked him.

Brady forced his gaze off Noelle. His head turned. He found Elliott regarding him with an intent stare. "You already know the answer to that."

More than anything. With all that I am.

"Yeah, I do." Elliott smiled. "Just like you already know you don't need my blessing, but you have it anyway." He motioned toward the stack of brightly wrapped packages under the tree. "Guessing the magical crew helped with those, too?"

"No." Brady's gaze had gone back to Noelle. "I went shopping."

"Damn." A whistle from Elliott. "And *that's* how much you love her. I shall assume a ring is in one of the boxes. Maybe in the tiny one?"

No, the tiny box held gold hoop earrings for Noelle. The engagement ring was in the biggest box. A box, within a box, within a box...because he wanted to see Noelle smile when she went through the packages and finally found the ring nestled deep inside.

Noelle's heels clicked across the hardwood floor. "You did all of this for me?"

"I'd do anything for you."

If possible, her smile beamed even brighter.

"God, that's sweet. Really. Sickeningly so, but I know Noelle will go for it, so it's obviously working for you." Elliott darted toward the entranceway. "On that note, I think I'll take my leave. I suspect you have some talking to do, presents to open...all that jazz." He paused. "I'm sorry about Addison and Rowen."

Noelle and Brady both turned to look at him.

Faint lines bracketed his mouth. "I brought them into our lives. I don't usually misjudge people that way."

"It's not your fault, Elliott," Noelle said.

"Then why do I feel like it is?" The lines deepened.

"Because you like to take the blame for too much." Noelle's hair slid over her shoulders. "This isn't on you. I don't blame you for anything. You're my brother, and I love you. I always will."

Hope flickered in his eyes as Elliott's gaze darted to Brady.

Sighing, Brady said, "Man, you know I don't blame you for a damn thing. You've had my back for years, and I will always have yours, too."

"So..." The shadow slid from Elliott's face. "For the record, I *am* gonna be the best man at the wedding then? I haven't lost my status?"

"You'll be the best man," Brady assured him.

"Good." A relieved sag of his shoulders. "Because I've been planning the bachelor party for the last week, and I would have hated to turn that beast over to someone else." He threw up a wave and headed for the door.

"The last week?" Noelle's brows rose as she studied Brady. "But you haven't even been in town for a week."

The front door closed behind Elliott.

Brady's hand slid under Noelle's chin. "True, but I've been in love with you forever." *And Elliott knew it all along.*

She crept closer to him. "Did you really decorate this place for me?"

In the interest of full disclosure, he told her, "A very skilled team of professionals decorated this place for you. I mostly supervised."

Her hand slid into her bag. "It's almost perfect."

Almost? His head whipped toward the tree. "Is it leaning too much? Dammit, was Elliott right about that?"

Her warm laughter wrapped around him. "The tree is great. I meant that you forgot one important thing."

He looked back at her and saw that she'd pulled something out of her purse.

"Mistletoe," Noelle whispered. "I don't see any in the room. Good thing I brought my own for us." She lifted it up.

It needed to be up a little higher, so he took it from her fingers. Held it over their heads. Under the mistletoe with Noelle. No hiding. No pretending. "I love you."

"I love you, too."

He could feel the smile sliding across his face, and Brady didn't know if he had ever been this happy before. But what he did know? *The rest of our lives will be like this.*

"Now go ahead and kiss me," Noelle said, her voice husky and sensual, "because this Christmas, you are all I want."

And he gave her just what she wanted. Brady kissed her.

THE END

Dear Reader

I love the holiday season. Each year, I try to write a new holiday tale because I think it is just such a magical time. Growing up, I would always eagerly count down the days until Christmas, and, of course, when Christmas finally came, I would be up long before the sun rose!

I hope that you enjoyed reading KISS ME THIS CHRISTMAS. I was able to include many of my favorite elements in this story (I adore a second chance romance!). Noelle and Brady were such a fun couple to write.

Happy reading,
Cynthia Eden
cynthiaeden.com

About the Author

Cynthia Eden is a *New York Times, USA Today, Digital Book World*, and *IndieReader* best-seller.

Cynthia writes sexy tales of contemporary romance, romantic suspense, and paranormal romance. Since she began writing full-time in 2005, Cynthia has written over one hundred novels and novellas.

Cynthia lives along the Alabama Gulf Coast. She loves romance novels, horror movies, and chocolate.

For More Information

- *cynthiaeden.com*
- *facebook.com/cynthiaedenfanpage*

Her other Works

Wilde Ways: Gone Rogue

- How To Protect A Princess (Book 1)

Ice Breaker Cold Case Romance

- Frozen In Ice (Book 1)
- Falling For The Ice Queen (Book 2)
- Ice Cold Saint (Book 3)
- Touched By Ice (Book 4)

Phoenix Fury

- Hot Enough To Burn (Book 1)
- Slow Burn (Book 2)
- Burn It Down (Book 3)

Trouble For Hire

- No Escape From War (Book 1)
- Don't Play With Odin (Book 2)
- Jinx, You're It (Book 3)
- Remember Ramsey (Book 4)

Death and Moonlight Mystery

- Step Into My Web (Book 1)
- Save Me From The Dark (Book 2)

Wilde Ways

- Protecting Piper (Book 1)
- Guarding Gwen (Book 2)
- Before Ben (Book 3)
- The Heart You Break (Book 4)
- Fighting For Her (Book 5)
- Ghost Of A Chance (Book 6)
- Crossing The Line (Book 7)
- Counting On Cole (Book 8)
- Chase After Me (Book 9)
- Say I Do (Book 10)
- Roman Will Fall (Book 11)
- The One Who Got Away (Book 12)
- Pretend You Want Me (Book 13)
- Cross My Heart (Book 14)
- The Bodyguard Next Door (Book 15)
- Ex Marks The Perfect Spot (Book 16)
- The Thief Who Loved Me (Book 17)

Dark Sins

- Don't Trust A Killer (Book 1)
- Don't Love A Liar (Book 2)

Lazarus Rising

- Never Let Go (Book One)
- Keep Me Close (Book Two)
- Stay With Me (Book Three)
- Run To Me (Book Four)
- Lie Close To Me (Book Five)
- Hold On Tight (Book Six)

Dark Obsession Series

- Watch Me (Book 1)
- Want Me (Book 2)
- Need Me (Book 3)
- Beware Of Me (Book 4)
- Only For Me (Books 1 to 4)

Mine Series

- Mine To Take (Book 1)
- Mine To Keep (Book 2)
- Mine To Hold (Book 3)
- Mine To Crave (Book 4)
- Mine To Have (Book 5)
- Mine To Protect (Book 6)
- Mine Box Set Volume 1 (Books 1-3)
- Mine Box Set Volume 2 (Books 4-6)

Bad Things

- The Devil In Disguise (Book 1)
- On The Prowl (Book 2)
- Undead Or Alive (Book 3)
- Broken Angel (Book 4)
- Heart Of Stone (Book 5)
- Tempted By Fate (Book 6)
- Wicked And Wild (Book 7)
- Saint Or Sinner (Book 8)
- Bad Things Volume One (Books 1 to 3)
- Bad Things Volume Two (Books 4 to 6)
- Bad Things Deluxe Box Set (Books 1 to 6)

Bite Series

- Forbidden Bite (Bite Book 1)
- Mating Bite (Bite Book 2)

Blood and Moonlight Series

- Bite The Dust (Book 1)
- Better Off Undead (Book 2)
- Bitter Blood (Book 3)
- Blood and Moonlight (The Complete Series)

Purgatory Series

- The Wolf Within (Book 1)
- Marked By The Vampire (Book 2)
- Charming The Beast (Book 3)
- Deal with the Devil (Book 4)
- The Beasts Inside (Books 1 to 4)

Bound Series

- Bound By Blood (Book 1)
- Bound In Darkness (Book 2)
- Bound In Sin (Book 3)
- Bound By The Night (Book 4)
- Bound in Death (Book 5)
- Forever Bound (Books 1 to 4)

Stand-Alone Romantic Suspense

- It's A Wonderful Werewolf
- Never Cry Werewolf
- Immortal Danger
- Deck The Halls
- Come Back To Me
- Put A Spell On Me
- Never Gonna Happen
- One Hot Holiday
- Slay All Day
- Midnight Bite
- Secret Admirer
- Christmas With A Spy

- Femme Fatale
- Until Death
- Sinful Secrets
- First Taste of Darkness
- A Vampire's Christmas Carol

Made in the USA
Monee, IL
02 December 2022

19213624R10079